ⓂORIGINALS

NEW WRITING FROM
BRITAIN'S OLDEST PUBLISHER

JM Originals is a new list from John Murray.
It is a home for fresh and distinctive new writing;
for books that provoke and entertain.

Generation

Paula McGrath

JM ORIGINALS

First published in Great Britain in 2015 by JM Originals
An imprint of John Murray (Publishers)
An Hachette UK Company

1

A version of 'Joe' was first published as 'Auslanders' in the *Ofi Press*;
'Yehudit' was first published in *Eclectica*, then in *Surge* (O'Brien Press, 2014).

A CIP catalogue record for this title is available from the British Library

Trade Paperback ISBN 978-1-47361-483-3
Ebook ISBN 978-1-47361-484-0

Typeset in Sabon MT by Palimpsest Book Production Limited,
Falkirk, Stirlingshire

Printed and bound by CPI Group (UK) Ltd, Croydon, CR0 4YY

John Murray policy is to use papers that are natural, renewable and
recyclable products and made from wood grown in sustainable forests.
The logging and manufacturing processes are expected to conform to the
environmental regulations of the country of origin.

John Murray (Publishers)
Carmelite House
50 Victoria Embankment
London EC4Y 0DZ

www.johnmurray.co.uk

For Othermammy

1958

You stand on the threshold of the pit you will enter and out of which you will not emerge for four full years. It's 1958. The Russians launched Sputnik into orbit last October and threw the Americans into a spin, so now they want uranium, badly. The Canadians can't get it out of the ground fast enough. That's why you're here, far from home. You're twenty-five years old. You know nothing about your future, about the woman you will marry, the children you will have: the flighty one, the solemn one, the one who will undo everything you are about to begin.

When you left school it wasn't a moment too soon. You hated the master. You wanted to be master of your own destiny. You were fourteen when you went to work in Duffy's. Fifteen miles on the bike there, another fifteen back, often with yesterday's newspaper tucked down the front of your coat to keep off the wind. You did that journey for years. On to England then with the rest, packing wool until you had your fill of that. With a toss of a coin you chose between Canada or Australia. Canada, the coin said, so you travelled home on the *Princess Maud* with Mick Carey and Charlie Ryan, *for the American wake*. They insisted. They were headed for New York. You'd travel with them that far. You had a week before you'd set sail.

On one of the last afternoons, you walked along the hedges of the fields you knew so well. You loved the land and hated it, too, for breaking your back with the stones you picked and the beet you thinned, for the ache in your legs from the miles you walked behind the plough, for the cold that went through you many a winter out there in the field, you wishing you were inside at the fire warming your feet.

You walked on, out in the lanes and boreens once you'd passed the boundary of your father's farm – Seán's now – not to be trespassing on another man's land. You followed a gentle incline, not enough to take the wind out of you, until you came to the copse, all that was left of the big house they burned

4

down before you were born: a few chestnuts and oaks, mossy stones and long grasses between.

It was the beginning of May, the loveliest time. You sat down and looked all about you, at the bright green young corn, and the *sceac* bushes dressed in lace; at the smoke coming from the cottages in thin grey curls, *the kettle on the hob/ Sing peace into his breast,* you remembered, Yeats. Even though you hated school, nearly every long minute of it, you liked the poems. Memorise every detail of the scene in front of you as if it's a poem, you told yourself, every line. You wanted to be able to take it out and look at it sometime when you might need it.

Lying back into the long grass, you looked up at the big chestnut leaves, lifting and fluttering like fingers in the breeze, bits of blue sky filtering between. *I think that I shall never see / A poem lovely as a tree,* and you thought, there is truth in that poem. You lay, completely still, until the hum and rustle of insects in the grass became loud as a city in your ears. You told yourself, remember the sounds, remember the touch of the breeze on your face, the gentle breath of your homeland.

On your way back, you shoved fistfuls of dirt into your pockets, furtively. Once you got inside you turned your pockets out into an old cigar tin you kept from Duffy's, then you pushed it deep down into your bag.

5

Your going-away party was a blur of whiskey and stout. The craic was mighty, the singing and the recitations, reminders of how many and how long Irish men and women had been leaving their own land. Threads of tunes ran one into the other, refrains of Mother Ireland, *ochón, ochón, Éire mo chroí*, until the night ran into day and the old men had far-away looks in their eyes. You wondered which bit of Ireland's tragic history they were thinking of. But there was a humming in your gut, too, pure excitement that the old men wouldn't understand. You were bursting to go, to see the world. But to admit this would be to betray your country, your people, these old men.

Besides, you'd be coming back, wouldn't you?

It was an old boat, and the passage rough and uncomfortable. You had more than a week of the Atlantic, and your fill of long-life food, what you could keep down. You were looking for it the whole way, New York, but when you set eyes on the Statue of Liberty with her arm in the air in greeting, you weren't ready. New York. The masses of people coming, people going, all shouting and pushing, all in a great big hurry. You couldn't stand still to take it all in because they'd knock you down. But you weren't there to see the sights. You said your goodbyes to Charlie and Mick, wondering if you'd ever see them again, then you asked for directions and got the bus to Parsippany, as far as your money stretched. Then you stuck out your thumb. A big black car driven by a tall and silent man brought you as far as Syracuse. A truck picked you up next. This man was a farmer. You got a bit of chat out of him. Couldn't believe it when you saw the signs to Liverpool. He laughed, told you London was further on, and Birmingham. There was even a Dublin, he thought, beyond in California or somewhere out west.

When you reached Buffalo he told you you were nearly there. It was just another few miles to Niagara. When you crossed the border from Niagara Falls, New York, into Niagara Falls, Ontario, you were completely thrown. You'd heard about the Falls, of course, but you weren't prepared for the sheer size of them, the crashing weight of the water, the deafening roar. Your own country was beautiful, an emerald isle. Here, you were to be the pining exile, far from the green grass of home. You didn't expect to have your breath taken away at the beauty of the foreign land. That wasn't the way of the old people's songs.

Canada. The space bewildered you. They called them lakes, but they were like oceans. Ontario, then Huron. Instinctively, you looked around for the highest hill, a Mount Leinster you could anchor yourself to, but here there were mountains, and you could sense the land stretching behind them, away out of your reach, as unimaginable as your future. You searched in vain for a horizon you could bring near you, fit around you like a jacket. The lack of boundaries unravelled you, you were drunk on it. You didn't know what to do with the feeling. The buzz of excitement that had sent you west, the feeling that anything might be possible, exploded out in all directions at once.

You stand on the threshold, in your hard hat with the lamp, and your overalls, thrumming the pickaxe in nervous readiness against your thigh. You look behind you one last time, out over the strange, barren landscape of Sudbury, with its scraggy few trees and blackened rock, then you punch your time card and step into the cage and go down. Daylight accompanies you the first few yards, then you're in the dark. The others switch on their lamps. You do the same.

You go down and down. When the cage opens you follow the ones who know where they're going, Ronnie, Jean, Albert, further and further into the black hole in the earth. Your boot keeps careful contact with one of the narrow gauge rails. The smell grows damp and earthy. You think of your cigar tin. The banter between the men helps take your mind off the mass of earth above your head as you go deeper and deeper.

Your eyes adjust to the dark. You like the monotony of the work: drawing back, stabbing the rock face, drawing back, stabbing. Ronnie uses a crowbar to loosen it up for you. There's a hose, for the dust, pulleys and ladders. There's a rhythm: your muscles flexing and extending and your breath keeping time. Each man on the crew has his own job, keeping time with the others. You work until lunch, when you come blinking to the surface to eat the breakfast you stuffed between two slices of bread – bacon, eggs, even the marmalade – on your way out of the boarding house that morning. You work from lunch until evening. If there's overtime, you take it: Christmas Day, Dominion Day, New Year's Day. When you're under the ground one day's the same as the next.

Once a week you queue for your wages. It's hard work but the pay is good. You go to the Algoden with the others – mining gives you a mighty thirst – but you put away the rest and stay in when the other lads go to the Snakepit. You're not doing this forever, just until you have enough. For now, you've swapped the sky for the underground world of men and money; open spaces for tunnels where your muscles are tense; fresh air and grass and rain for beery farts and unwashed bodies. You get used to it. When you emerge

9

out of the up-cage it's not much better. There are nearly no trees, and nothing green. You come out of the black hole in the rock to look at a landscape of black rocks. It's a view made by the mining, and from cutting the trees down for fuel. You don't know about acid rain but you have a fair idea why the sparkle in the granite rocks has been eaten up all around the mines. They remind you of the decayed, pitted teeth of the old people at home. You make sure to take extra care with yours, brushing them twice a day with salt and bread soda to keep them strong and white. Girls you've met in the past at dances have admired your smile. Later, you'll keep on doing it that way, even when you have your choice of fluoride this and minty that, along with showers instead of baths, the habits you'll bring back.

There are days, looking out across the minescape, when you'd have given anything to be lying under a chestnut. Other days, you step out of the boarding house and look off across Elliot Lake, and you love the way there's no end to it, the way it makes you feel you can really breathe. You pick the blueberries that grow wild on the sides of the road in the acidic soil and they seem like a luxury compared to the common blackberries of your childhood.

You get used to it.

One morning there's Albert, the German, saying, *Come, come. I teach you to skate.* It's a strange skill for an Irishman. You'd prefer a good game of football. At home, you made it as far as the Carlow Seniors subs bench, and you miss it out here. When the thaw comes you kick a soccer ball around with Ronnie and Albert, but your instinct to scoop up the ball and run with it is too strong and they shout at you to *Put it down, Paddy*. It feels like half a game to you. You doubt you could ever get used to it.

You and the other foreigners go along with the sled races, the skating tricks, the swimming and diving in the lake. On summer Sundays, a few of you take the wrapped sandwiches and apples your landlady makes for you and head out of Sudbury, into the country.

Once, you splash out and take a train, far into the wild. You pass lake after lake – there are three hundred of them in the area – then you get off, miles from anywhere. You stand and listen. You think about the wildlife the woods are harbouring. Badgers and hares and rabbits, like at home, but you know there are moose and deer too, even black bears, and wild cats. You listen. It gives you an edge of fear, a thrill of excitement. You ask yourself if you could live here, work the land in ways that are unfamiliar to you. In the papers you read about the acres you could buy for the price of a small farm at home. Could you get used to it?

You don't like the long winter. Nothing could have

prepared you for those minus temperatures which no amount of woollen socks or layers can compensate for. But there's the snow and ice to compensate, the beauty that even Sudbury takes on when it's under a thick white cover. And it's not the winter that's the worst, it's the humid heat of the summer. There's no comfort to be had in the damn heat. You can take off your shirt and roll your trousers but you're still sweating. The English and Germans and Italians lie out in it on Sundays, getting brown, but you're ahead of your time, convinced you should keep your pale skin covered. After your shift you swim in the lake to escape it, but there's no peace even at night. You can't sleep with the heat.

You break out in a homesick sweat one night, your skin remembering the light, cool breeze. You lift the lid off your tin, just a corner, and the cool musky smell near breaks your heart.

You had a letter from your oldest sister, the one who was like another mother to you, with the age gap, pretending all innocence. *I happened to bump into Anne. You remember Mick's niece, don't you . . .* But there was nothing innocent about it. You laughed at the idea, Margaret setting you up with a girl from Ballon, and you over here in Canada. All the same, you find yourself keeping an eye on the *Land for Sale* section in the *Nationalist* when Margaret sends it over.

There's days off sometimes, when the mine is closed altogether. There's always something planned. You join Ronnie and Albert and hitchhike all the way to Chicago. The Windy City. You have no problem getting lifts. The locals like the lads from the mine. They're good for business. You're in the back of the pick-up when you round Lake Ontario and cross into the United States, and there's a bastard of a wind coming down across the lake. None of you dressed warm enough and you're frozen stiff when you arrive.

You stand where you're dropped off, rubbing your hands together and stomping your feet while you make plans. Albert wants to travel on the elevated trains; Ronnie wants to see the new Inland Steel skyscraper. You want to go to the famous Marshall Field's. Margaret read about it in a women's magazine and mentioned it in her letter, how she'd give anything to see it. You split up. You ask a fellow where State Street is and he points you in the right direction. It's something all right. You've never seen a shop the size of it, or as fancy, not even in Dublin or Liverpool. The Yanks like to do things big. Even the doorman is fancy, in a uniform, like something out of a film. You ask him where you would go to find a wedding present. He suggests the homeware department. You think you recognise his accent. *Are you from Chicago yourself?* you ask him. He laughs. *No one's from*

Chicago, he says. *It's Louth I'm from.* He calls a boy and tells him to take over, and he walks you through all the counters. You're dazzled by the lotions and potions, but all he wants is to talk about the football, and you're happy to do it, Louth and its two-point win over Cork. Not your counties, but you love the game. You don't know, nor does this Louthman, that it will be the last time for above sixty years that they take the title. With obvious reluctance he leaves you at last in the hands of a swanky shop assistant and tells her to treat you right.

She asks what she can do for you, so you tell her about your younger sister, Theresa, getting married in the autumn, and that you're looking for something nice for a present. She asks what kind of budget you had in mind. You tell her you just want something nice, a bit special. You like the feel of the wad of cash in your trousers. She has all the time in the world for you. In the end you settle on a canteen of silver cutlery. She tells you it's a very popular present with brides this year. At the cash register you throw in a couple of boxes of Frango mints for Margaret's kids.

You meet up with your gang and you go to a restaurant for dinner, a treat. You can't believe the size of the steak they put in front of you. You have a drink after. Ronnie has heard about dance halls where you can pay a ticket-a-dance for a beautiful girl to dance with you, and he plans to get completely soaked and dance all night. You won't join him, you tell him. You're buying a farm. He laughs, *Paddy's buying a farm*. He's just having a bit of fun. You decide you'll join him after all, just to keep him company.

When you get back to Sudbury and fall in the door of the boarding house barely in time to get out of your good clothes and into your overalls, your landlady hands you a telegram. *Father passed away Stop Funeral tomorrow Stop Will write Stop.*

Margaret's letter comes a couple of weeks later. Old Seán, as your father was known, had died peacefully in his sleep. The funeral went off well. But she was wondering. Theresa was wondering. Would there be any chance at all you could come home for the wedding, to give her away? Mick's niece would be there . . .

When you surface from your man-made midnight into day, and punch your card for the last time, you don't know that in just a few years astronauts will travel to Sudbury's lunar landscape to learn about meteorites, and the Americans will land a man on the moon. You don't know that many years later a Canadian will tweet from space while he orbits the earth, sending back unimaginable views of your green land. You don't know that one day this mine you're walking away from for the last time will become Elliot Lake Nuclear Mining Museum, that tourists will find your name in the List of Miners on the wall.

Spring 2010

Joe

Sheets of rain on the windshield. Wipers can't keep up. The faithful Dead for company. *Twisted. Broken.* Thick, furred, out of practice, can't remember the last time he spoke. Some girl on Skype. Vietnam? No, China. Stutters and starts. Non-starter. No English. No connection. Next.

A dirty brown sludge at the side of the road, all that's left of the snow. The drip-drip-drip from the roof is what brings each spring to him, his wake-up call, his thaw. Get up. Get out. Get stocked up. Hurry. Make a list. Lists. Where's the list? He riffles through the open glove compartment. He put it right here. Where is it? Now what? What was on his list? Early start. He can't remember. Late last night he was full of ideas. Murky half-memories now. Goddamn.

He hates the city. City boy, hates it now. Super early, so no one's on the road. He'll get in before the wholesaler's open. Grab a coffee at the gas station on the way. A gnaw somewhere deep reminds him of hunger, led by the body, the real deal. He nods at the recognition, in rhythm with the music; he's super hungry. It's been a while. It's that time of year again all right. He'll get one of their awesome hotdogs. The right toppings, plenty of the green sauce, hit the spot. Couple of dollars. You can keep your fancy restaurants.

Should be an email waiting when he gets back. Six hours ahead. Calculates, it's . . . eleven thirty there, she's at work. *I love the outdoors, nature, growing things*, yada-yada. At least she speaks English.

Slap of tyres on the tarmac. Black rain, black sky. No line separating the one from the other. Tell her that. *Couldn't make out where the road ended and the sky began.* She seems to like that poetic shit.

Each of her emails sounds like a résumé, with a shitload of flirting thrown in. *I love picking fruit. I picked strawberries every summer when I was growing up. I really love that photo where you're picking peppers.* That's the one where he has his shirt off. They all go for that one. *Are your eyes really that brown?* Reckon she fits somewhere between wwoofer and online dater. She'd clean up the house at least. It looks like shit. Always does, this time of year. Last year's woman got it into some kind of order.

He'll ease off on the weed. He's out now anyway. Rolled the last joint last night. Won't let the same thing happen next fall. No way. This time he'll be ready. He'll go to the mountains. Take a hike. Start juicing. Get healthy again. Make some changes around the farm. Lose the beard. Meet someone.

He's pretty sure she's not the one. But she'll fill the gap. Someone to talk to. Divorced with a kid. They're always the neediest, always the top of his list. He'll ask her. Ask her today. Come on over, check out the farm. Bring your kid. Throw it in, casual.

For maybe a mile he's optimistic. Hell, he'll call her up. Surprise her. Get her all set up on Skype. Wonder what her voice sounds like?

He wonders what his own voice sounds like. Winters are hard. Send him down into himself. He can't seem to help it. Soon as he smells the rot of fall, he's gone. The woodiness, the mould, it fills him full of holes. When the fall air starts to blow right through him he knows it's time to retreat. Hide away in his smoky den to hold himself together. He gives a short laugh. Her needy could never match his needy. Driving like this, on his own, sometimes he thinks he's so full of holes he could just fall apart.

Sing it, Phil. Ah, good ol' Gerry. That was the

Soldier Field gig. 'Ninety-five – or was it six? That was one heck of a gig. 'Box of Rain'. Which box to put this one in? Works in an office. Seen the photos. Skirts and nylons, that bullshit. Looks a bit lame. Not a worker. Wait. Will she even be home from work when he gets back? She has to be. He needs her to be. Needs someone, anyone. She's the only one he's written to this year, if he doesn't count the Chinese. He only had energy for one. Pulling it out of himself, the lines, through his fingertips into his emails, lines she'll want to read. It worked. She was hooked. He can tell by now, the ones who're worth his while. He calculates. He sent his mail before he left. Sent another before he dozed off. And one before that. And . . . OK, so he sent a few. She must've been busy. Sleeping. The kid. Whatever. He checked, um, twenty times, more? No reply. *No New Mail* freaks him out. His breath gets shorter, fast. Even thinking about it. She should have replied by the time he gets back though. Surely?

His hands prickle with perspiration. He tries to ignore his racing pulse. Least thing sets it off when he quits the weed. One of his hands leaves the steering wheel of its own accord. It's patting his pants leg, the pocket on the thigh, the hip. The other side. Where he keeps a small emergency stash. Just to get through it. There . . . There you are, you little beauty. He eases out the plastic coin-bag. Glances down.

Sweet. A bit dusty, but enough for one last joint. Make it last. A few more hours, get him over the worst. Roll it at the gas station, he's thinking, but he's already feeding the wheel clockwise through his hands and the van is crossing over into the emergency lane and slowing.

His hands are shaking but they are well practised and in no time he has the paper between his lips, the car lighter at the other end, and he is pulling the pungent smoke into his lungs. Already the dirty graveyard-hour has lightened to predawn grey, and now the jagged edges of his mind begin to soften. He sings along with the Dead. Hell, there's that darn list, over there on the dashboard the whole time. How'd he miss it before?

He chuckles quietly to himself as he pulls back into traffic.

Carlos

Silvia and his youngest are arguing inside. Tia does not speak with respect. Carlos does not know how to deal with her. His first girl, Rosa, comes every day, she kisses her Mama and her Papa, she helps in the kitchen, she serves lunch, she kisses them again when she goes back to her husband. She is a good girl. *I missed you, Papa,* she always said when he came back each year. *I miss you, Papa,* she says still. When she was little she followed him around everywhere, when he was home.

In the middle is his serious Isabel. She always has her head in a book, always studying.

—I want to go to high school, Papa. I want to go to college. I'm going to be a lawyer when I grow up. I'm going to go to the United States and be a lawyer.

—Then I will retire good, he told her. I will retire early and go live with my daughter, the big shot lawyer. But before you become a lawyer, how about you kiss your Papa?

He has to remind this one. She has too many books, too many words in her head. He didn't believe she would be a lawyer. Children say these things. But here she is, his daughter, a student in U de G, studying law, when he himself did not even finish grade school. It makes him feel proud, like he made the right decision, always away from home, always working.

This time she tells him she will not emigrate. She will stay here, in Guadalajara. She tells him Mexico needs its educated young people. Besides, she wants to be here to take care of her Mama and her Papa when they get old.

—I am old already, he tells her.

—No you're not, Papa, she says, kissing his forehead. But you work too hard.

Hard work he learned from his father. As a child he went to school for the morning session, then he would take his lunch to the river and sit under a tree in the shade, listen to the frogs and cicadas until their clicks and low rumbles sent him into a torpor, only to stretch himself awake when the main heat of the sun was gone. Then it was time to help his father. No rushing. No panic. Have lunch, then siesta. Then work. Work in the fields until the light was all gone. No matter if the muscles grew tired.

Not like the gringo. He is always rushing, always panicking. The five-year plans, the crop-rotation charts, the accounts. But then, he lies in his bed for two hours after the sun comes up, finishes the day at five o'clock. How does that make sense? He is no farmer, that is for sure. Carlos thinks he is a little bit crazy. Harmless crazy, but you never know. He has dumb ideas: Carlos, do this, Carlos, do that. *Yes, sir*, he says, even though it is crazy. Fence this, dig that, pipe this, it takes a week, three weeks, six weeks. Doesn't matter. At the end of each week, he gets a wad of dollars from the crazy hippy gringo, takes it to Western Union in Rockford, and sends most of it to Silvia.

He doesn't need much for himself. His room: bed, bedside table, a box where he keeps his clothes. He has his pictures of Silvia, the girls. It is always a shock when he goes back and the girls no longer look like their pictures. He feels as if they have cheated him. Do they feel the same? He thinks he is a stranger to them, he tells Silvia. To Tia especially. He doesn't know how to talk to her. Silvia says it's because sixteen is a difficult age. She is always at a

26

difficult age, it seems to Carlos. But what does he know. He is never there.

At the start the gringo wanted Carlos to live at the farm, sleep in one of the bedrooms. Bad idea, the worst of ideas, but the gringo did not see this. *Great idea*, he says. *It'd be great, my man. Save rent, save gas. Bring your family here.* He talks fast. Drive anyone crazy, like him. *My man. Bring your family.* Carlos' mouth tightens. Silvia would not like what she would see there. It is filthy, everywhere filthy. The idea of bringing his wife, who will not sit until everything is scrubbed white, swept clean. It is an insult, telling him to bring his family. The man lives worse than a dog. Alone. Never sees his own family, but wants some other family to live in his house with him. The gringo's father, he comes out to the farm in his fancy car. Money there. An only child, too. He tries, he asks how things work. *What's new?* he asks. It is hard, talking to your children when they grow up. They do not want to talk to you anymore. The gringo ignores his father, acts like he's insulted, like his father is spying on him. *What's new?* the father asks, and the gringo turns his back, walks away to the hoophouses, leaves his father standing there, helpless, a man trying to be a father to his son.

An invisible band around Carlos' chest tightens. No, he does not want to think about fathers, sons.

Not today. Not when he is about to leave again. He will deal with that another day, every other day.

Inside the house the voices are raised.

—It is your father's last night . . .

—He won't care.

—*I* care, Letitia.

A door slams.

Silvia is the one who holds the family together, keeps everyone on track in school, at home, at church, keeps them fed and healthy, makes all the decisions. She is a strong woman. She has to be, when he is not here. When he is here, she tries to act like he is the head of the house. He tries to go along with it, but they are not good at pretending.

She comes out to the porch and sits beside him.

—Tia wants to go to the Spring Break dance with her school friends. Some boy will be there.

—It's tonight?

—Mm hm. Tonight.

—It's OK, Silvia – he begins.

—It's *not* OK, Carlos, Silvia interrupts. It's not OK for your daughter to go out with her friends when her father is leaving for six months. Besides, I don't like the sound of this boy.

He hears in her voice that she is thinking about another time, another leaving. She is thinking, is this the last time? Is this the time he won't come back?

Antonio did not want to stay in Guadalajara, become a drone for IBM or HP. He wanted to travel, see something of the world. He wanted adventure.

—Come to Chicago, Carlos told his nephew Antonio when he complained about school. He had turned seventeen the week before, same as Rosa. They celebrated their birthdays together, Antonio and Rosa, always letting Tia cheat with the piñata. Already seven years ago now.

Already, he'd had adventures with the graffiti, and a gang of boys his father, Carlos' brother Ramón, did not like. Ramón was worried Antonio was falling in with a bad crowd. Today it's graffiti, tomorrow it's drugs, gangs, guns. *Come to Chicago. There is plenty of work.* Why, why did he encourage him?

Silvia was unhappy.

—What is wrong with clean, easy work, good pay? Here, near his family.

—Let him get it out of his system, Carlos said. Some good hard work in the fields, or in the factories. It will make him happy to work for the IBMs.

He was pleased with himself, with his plan for his nephew.

Antonio. He could have stayed, with Ramón and

29

his mother and his brothers. He would be safe there now, if Carlos had not encouraged him.

—Why, Papa, why did you take Antonio away? the then nine-year-old Tia demanded when he came back, when he told them what had happened. Why did you take away my cousin?

She was pounding on his chest, tears and snot running down her face.

The desert, scrubby, dry, the sky a searing white-blue. The air hums with heat. A lizard darts under a rock nearby. They must wait, in whatever shade they can find. Carlos knows how the boy's heart is pounding, that it is adrenaline alone that keeps it pumping. It is dangerous, but Carlos has done the crossing several times by now, knows how much you have to pay the Coyote, knows if you play by their rules they will get you there safely. Fifteen hundred each up front, fifteen hundred when the job is done. Don't make trouble, and you don't get trouble. They might be gangsters, but they are also businessmen. He tells Antonio this while they wait.

—It's cool, Uncle, Antonio says. But his eyes are darting, his muscles tensed.

It will be good for him, Carlos thinks, this border crossing. It is dangerous, but let him call it adventure if he wants adventure. Then the hard work, the dull, hard work. He will return home and go straight into a college course before summer ends.

They wait until the sun makes red gashes across the darkening sky, then they make a run for the river.

Carlos has a visa now. The gringo fixed it for him. This evening he will take the faded yellow-and-green bus, arrive at Tijuana after many hours of half-sleep and terrible dreams. He will jolt awake, soaked in sweat. Silvia would prefer him to fly. Flying is as cheap, maybe even cheaper. Not so hard on him. But when he is not sleeping Carlos likes to see the blue of the Pacific out his window, the stony Sierra Madres out the other. He likes to fix them inside his head in case he does not make it back again. He does not try to explain to Silvia, just buys his ticket; she does not try to change his mind. When he gets to Tijuana, he will walk through the checkpoint, show them his visa, cross the border. Still, he will feel like he is committing a crime.

His first years in the United States he worked as a day labourer. Avocados, oranges, corn. Staying in bunkhouses with six or ten or more, moving with the seasons, further north as the year moved on, then back to Mexico in October. It was rough living. He tried not to tell her too much, but Silvia did not like the little she knew of it. He found work in LA, in a meat-packing factory, shared a room with two others he never saw because they all worked crazy shifts. The money was good, but he missed the fields, so when his cousin told him about Chicago, he moved north. The cost of living was cheap so he could send more home to Silvia. He found work with a farm contractor, a big operation. Up and down thousand-acre fields. It was better than the factory.

After Antonio, when he heard about work on a small organic farm up in the corner of Illinois, he drove straight out there. It was tiny, labour intensive, all day spent planting, weeding, harvesting. Hard work, but it brought a kind of peace. All day his mind on nothing but the perfection of the Sun Gold tomatoes in his palm, the scent of Thai basil rubbed between his fingers.

Perfect if it wasn't for the gringo. The day he drove out, Carlos spent twenty minutes nodding while the gringo talked at high speed. His vision, his dreams, his ambitions. What's wrong with farming today. How we lost touch with the land, with what we eat. On and on. He took Carlos by surprise when he finally finished; he had long stopped listening.

—What do you say? Want to come on board? Join our family? Twelve bucks an hour, cash. After the first season you get a raise.

Join the family? As far as Carlos could tell, he lived in the big, half-rotten house by himself. Twelve. It was two bucks more than he got now. Cash.

—*Sí*. Yes, I take the job.

He quickly figured out that nodding was the easiest thing. There was much talk, how to prepare for the season, for the week, for the day, for the market, but Carlos did not need to listen. He nodded, agreed. Turned a blind eye when he had to. Kept to himself. Took his lunch behind the barn to get some peace from the gringo. From the young workers too. Students, most of them, talking loudly, playing their music. And *wwoofers*. This word was new. So was the idea. World-wide opportunities on organic farms. These people, from far away across the world: Germany, England, Australia, other places he did not know. They stayed in the house with the gringo, even the girls. Some of them tried to straighten the place out. Made food for him too. None of them ever lasted long. When the gringo couldn't understand why, Carlos remarked that he was not surprised since they worked for nothing. The gringo narrowed his eyes at this. Carlos knew by now how unpredictable he could be. Flew into rages over nothing. He had seen him fire a student for dropping trash. The kid said it was an accident. Didn't matter. It was best not to cross him.

By October they're all gone anyway, except for Carlos. He will finish up loose ends around the farm, put equipment into storage, make repairs, leave when the snows start. By then the gringo is sitting in the small room, the den, he calls it, all day and night, watching TV, smoking. Eats when he gets the hunger, chips, pretzels, snacks, no real food. Drinks coffee after coffee, leaves the mugs everywhere, uses them for ashtrays. Dredges of sludge in the bottom. Makes Carlos sick when he goes up there to get paid. Smoking, smoking, smoking. When the snow comes in hard, Carlos thinks he probably doesn't move at all. Doesn't shave either. Looks like a bear crawling out of hibernation by the time Carlos' car comes slushing up the driveway in the thaw. Every spring, Carlos crosses the border, takes buses to Chicago and then to Rockford, picks up his old Ford Taurus and drives out to the farm, and while he is driving there he is never sure if it will still be there.

Antonio is a good swimmer, but it is not about swimming, it is about trying to stay low, trying not to fall over rocks, not to splash.

—Nearly there, Carlos calls in a loud whisper over the racket of the water.

Antonio is downriver, by now an outline against the dark mauve sky. He makes a brave attempt at a thumbs up. Then they are scrambling out on the other side. They rest a moment to catch their breath on the bank of the Rio Grande. Antonio is panting hard. Carlos knows it's from fear, not exertion.

—How's this for adventure, hey? he tries.

—Where are they? Antonio is looking around. Ramón insisted that he use his savings for the crossing, and 750 of Antonio's own dollars have already gone to the Coyote. He handed it over himself.

—They'll be here any minute.

Even as he says it, they hear the approaching engine, then they see the outline of a pick-up coming towards them, no lights. They run towards it and climb in. The driver sticks out his hand.

—You pay the balance.

He looks about the same age as Carlos, Mexican too.

—When we get to the border.

Antonio surprises Carlos with his bravery as well as his stupidity. This is no time for playing macho games.

—Pay or get out, the driver replies.

Carlos has already noticed the smooth wood and metal sticking out of the man's pocket. He has his own money ready. He nudges Antonio with his elbow. Slowly, Antonio pulls the plastic bag out of his hiking boot. The driver snatches it and revs up the engine, and soon they are rattling and jolting across the desert.

They have gone only a few hundred yards when suddenly everything is chaos. There are lights coming from everywhere, more pick-ups. The driver has leaned across them and opened their door while the truck is still moving. He is bawling at them,

—Get out!

They are too stunned to move.

—Immigration! Out!

Carlos is half-pushing, half-dragging Antonio, who still has not moved. Now Carlos is screaming too,

—Get out!

—Not until he gives me back my money.

There is pushing, pulling, shouting. Now there are flashing lights, more shouting.

A gunshot.

Antonio stops resisting. A last push from the driver. Carlos is on the ground, Antonio is beside him, limp. The pick-up roars away, followed by another and another, sending up a rain of rocks. A man in uniform is shining a flashlight on the surprise fixed on Antonio's face.

You don't want to move a muscle in this middle-of-the-day heat. It's cooler in the house. Silvia keeps all the shades drawn. There's even A/C now, though she rarely turns it on

—For emergencies, she says when the girls try to get round her.

36

But they both prefer to sit outside, on the porch, letting their gaze rest idly on nothing in particular across the street.

It feels like yesterday that they first moved in. They sat on the porch then, too, the new mortgage papers from the bank inside, on top of the few boxes they had brought with them from the apartment. Their first house, with a yard for Rosa and Isabel to play in. They had three bedrooms, a kitchen and a lounge, instead of the two rooms they rented downtown. They even had their own porch, and a porch bench, courtesy of Ramón, a house-warming present. Ramón had managed to buy a house the year before, just a few streets over. He told them about the new subdivision, how much better it was than the city, how there were playgrounds for the children, neighbourhood stores, like in their home town. How happy his three boys were. All their children would be able to play together. That first night, sitting side by side, they didn't need to tell each other how happy they were.

Many of the households up and down the street, in the next street, all through the subdivision, are run by women, their men, like Carlos, gone for most of the year. The front yard across the street has nothing but dust and dead grass and faded toys. Many different families have lived there over the years. It's rented out now.

Sylvia keeps their own yard as neat as she keeps

the house. Not a leaf out of place, at least not for long. The avocado tree has grown so big its shade even reaches the porch. Like many others, they had to make sacrifices, but they are among the lucky ones. This fall, Silvia made the last payment to the bank. Now, filed away carefully by her, they have the deeds to the house.

—You will be OK, Silvia?

He does not need to look to know that she nods.

Of course. I have been OK for sixteen years. Why would I not be OK this time?

Yes, he thinks. *She will be OK.* Still, he has Tia on his mind. This one is wilful. He does not say. He does not want to put a voice to Silvia's fear.

They sit in easy silence. He does not want to think about saying goodbye in a few hours. It is always hard. It gets harder, not easier.

—Maybe this will be the last crossing, he says. Maybe next spring I will stay home.

Carlos does not look at his wife. He is afraid he might see her eyes wide open in surprise. He is surprised himself. How long has he thought this? A winter, then a summer, then another winter, all in Guadalajara, with his wife, with Isabel, with Tia. With Rosa and her husband a short drive away, maybe a baby soon, a grandchild. He tries to imagine what this life might be like, what he would do, how he would spend his days.

He cannot. He knows only work, rising and retiring with the sun. And what about Silvia? Having him home would change everything for her. The life she knows is a life without a man-of-the-house, a man in the house. When she does not say anything, and he can bear it no longer, he half-turns to face her and he is touched to see a tear on her cheek. A tear, but she is smiling. Even after all these years, even after three children, she is still beautiful. Her hair, like his, has many greys, her face has lines. But she is still beautiful to him. He touches the wetness on her cheek with his finger. He wants his wife now as much as ever he wanted her.

Three bells ring out across the rooftops from Saint Joseph's. From the house, quick footsteps approach. The screen door opens. Tia, with her hair wrapped in a towel, smelling of apples.

—The food is all set, Mama. I need to finish getting ready for Mass.

She hesitates, turns back towards them.

—We'll have a special dinner together, Papa. I'll stay home. I'm sorry, Papa.

She bends and kisses him, and then she is gone with a bang and a clatter. He takes Silvia's hand and holds it until the screen door finally stops thudding and the quiet settles around them in folds.

Joe

The new woman, Áine – *awn-ya*, he thinks – takes off across the park in search of the Coffee Monkey. As he watches her go he sees a couple approach from North Clark, with another state-of-the-art stroller. Lincoln Park is full of them. In Chicago you don't forget that brown slush and six-foot drifts are never far behind and never far away. These two are not enjoying themselves. She's holding her arms across her chest, a slight woman with slouched shoulders. He's large and fair-haired, pushing the stroller towards the stall, a determined look on his face. He's too tall for the stroller, which gives him an awkward gait.

—That's eighteen dollars to you. Enjoy. Yes, sir, give it a try and taste the difference yourself. It's super fresh. All organic. No pesticides, no artificial fertilisers. Mother Nature, the way she should be. Thank you, sir. And your change. Can I help you, ma'am?

He's the snake-oil man, with his fast talk and quick sales. As they get closer he can hear that they are speaking German. Bickering in German. *You're the one who . . . You're always . . .*

He didn't know he could speak it until he went to college. Sounded like an easy credit: German for Beginners. He'd known a few words. Only, when he got to class he discovered he knew more than a few; he was fluent. Crazy. Mom was supposed to speak English to him. Dad was emphatic. No son of his was gonna be an ignorant immigrant, going around talking pidgin English. It was time to *fuggedabout all that*. War. Camps. Dad didn't want to know about Mom's *all that*. But Dad was out all day selling used cars, so Mom spoke German with him by day then switched to English at dinner, until he started school. He got his easy credit from a sceptical college teacher, but beyond that it changed nothing. He never even mentioned it to his mom. For all he knew, she forgot how to speak it herself.

The stroller has a cup holder and three wheels, the type you see with parents who jog, though the parents don't look like the jogging type. The baby is large and sweaty-headed, asleep.

—Hi there. What can I do you folks for?

The man steers the buggy out of the way and moves the reluctant woman forward in front of him, his mouth twisted unpleasantly.

—You are the one who only eats organic. A joke, since you don't eat anything at all, do you, Katja?

He leaves her stranded there and walks away with the stroller towards the playground, though the baby is too young for the rides.

She looks embarrassed, but manages a little laugh and a shrug, as if things would be fine if she could only pretend they were. He has to give her credit for that.

—Can I help? he asks, less the showman.

—Just . . . some vegetables, she says, with her accent.

When she smiles her teeth seem too large for her mouth.

—What is in season?

She doesn't seem to notice the boxes of peppers and tomatoes and squash between them, laid out in oranges and reds, yellows and greens.

—For you, Lollo Rosa, Cut-and-Come-Again, Romaine . . . He has it down.

—I'm sorry. I did not catch the second?

—Cut-and-Come-Again. You just pick what you want for your salad . . . Are you a salad girl?

She's not, at least not in a real, hearty way, great shovelfuls on the side with a beef-steak. You get a good appetite farming. Not this one. She's the pick-at-salad-and-call-it-dinner type. You can tell by her thin wrists, her pallor. She's unconsciously twisting her wedding band on her finger. She sees him watching.

—I might be, she says, lowering her hands and looking directly at him for the first time. I like very fresh.

He raises an eyebrow. She answers by shaking back her hair and straightening her shoulders, thrusting small breasts forward in her blouse. The kind of blouse, ironed, with a collar, that his Mom used to wear when she could still fit into regular clothes.

She looks like she needs taking care of. Her guy has had enough, it seems.

—You know what's good for you, he says. He emphasises the first *you*.

He holds her gaze. He's a good-looking guy, he has been told often enough, with his deep brown eyes, his fit body. His Farmers' Market neighbours give him a hard time, say it's why he makes so many sales, chatting up the ladies. But he's not like that. He makes no effort to impress, wears his clothes to bed for days at a time, weeks, sometimes. He doesn't bother with shaving, and he cuts his own hair when it starts to annoy him. He is more into a good worker, the stronger, more weathered, the better, than one of these insipid girlies who stroll around the park at weekends. If they want to interpret everything as flattery and flirtation it's not his fault.

—Here, try.

He holds out a handful of Sun Golds. She puts her hand lightly under his as if it needs steadying while she chooses. Coquettish. He can feel a tingle where she has made sure to stroke her finger as she picks the yellow fruit out of the centre of his palm. He can feel his dislike growing. He knows what comes next. She smells, gives a little coo, examines. Mouth open, tongue protruding, just a little. Hesitates. Pops it in. Closes her eyes to heighten the experience as she bursts the skin, and juice and seeds fill her mouth.

—Mm. It is sweet as candy, she breathes, looking at him as she eats, very slowly.

It's a fucking tomato, lady.

Her husband has come back, but she hasn't noticed yet. Joe moves away to other customers, leaves them to it, but he can hear the poisonous gutturals from the other side of the stall. The man is saying something colloquial. It must be the *verboten* subject because she jolts back as if he has hit her, shrinks back into her blouse, into her hair. He guesses; it's how he occupies his time, tending the market stall. An affair, probably. Texts full of longing and stroking, then the

44

clandestine couplings. Then – ba-ba-ba-boom – she's pregnant, accident, design, whatever. They're stuck now. He's as tired of them as they are of each other, wants them gone. He drifts back to where they are standing.

—The lettuces are on sale, since it's getting late in the day. There's a special on the Beefs too. Make a swell salad with mozzarella and basil, drizzle of olive oil. Smell.

Because other customers are listening, they obediently finger and sniff his produce. Sometimes he thinks he wants it for himself – he glances towards the barber-striped canopy of the Coffee Monkey where Áine has gone – the walks, coffees, conversations in bed, the sex. Then he gets reminded what it's really like. Makes him think of his parents. Dad shouting at night, Mom acting like everything is fine in the morning. As if kids are deaf, and dumb.

The couple has moved away to the basils.

—Think we can manage to take care of a few plants? she asks her husband.

—Sure, maybe the minder could water them.

There's something in his tone, even though he is smiling. She shoots him a glance.

—I can—

—When you're home?

—I'm home. She lowers her voice again but the flash of anger has made her audible. When I can—

—Not exactly stay-at-home-mum. *Rabenmutter.*
He spits the German word for raven, the bird that
abandons its young, the word for working mothers
in the *old country.*

—We could never afford . . . Your maintenance . . .

—So we pay someone to mind our child. And our
basil.

She knows he is listening to them, even though
she does not know he can understand German.

—Then leave the infernal basil, she says in
exasperation.

Guess the spring stroll in the park is not working
out.

—Yes. Leave the infernal basil. The infernal child
too. Because Katja has to go to work.

He does the inverted comma thing when he says
it, *arbeit*, work. The gloves are really coming off
now.

Áine is back with coffee. He sees that she is taking
in the couple, him. She knows something is up.

—Hey. He takes a coffee. Long line at the
Monkey, huh?

She kisses him, keeping one eye on the German
girl. Staking a claim.

—It's crowded enough, all right. Were you busy
here?

He can hear the edge. Wants to know what exactly
is going on. Already.

46

—Yeah. Want to handle this one? They're shopping for basil.

A test. Unfair, he knows. Heck, it's only her third day in the country. Her reconnaissance, as she insists on calling it. At first she doesn't know what to do with her coffee. But then she finds a crate under the table. Good for her. He turns and pretends an interest in two ladies choosing cut flowers, a sideline last year's woman started.

—Beautiful sunflowers, ladies. Brighten up the lounge.

Áine starts telling the Germans about the basils. The Thai and the Lemon, the Purple Bush, the Cinnamon, the Greek, Holy Basil, rattling them off in that funny Irish accent, even the ones missing their labels.

—The Sweet. This one is really easy to grow. Just pick off the stars as they come. They're great for the freezer.

He didn't know you could freeze it. Maybe this one has a few surprises for him after all.

The couple is at an impasse. She can't buy plants because she is never home to care for them. But she can't not because she has invested too much in this already, and everyone is watching, including him. Áine is waiting. At a loss at what to do, the woman pretends to attend to the baby, who is still asleep. All conversation and commerce at the Farm Fresh stand is momentarily suspended, all eyes are on them. At last the husband snatches the nearest plant and throws dollars on the table.

Áine glances over to where she knows he is watching, delighted with her first sale.

Yehudit

Judy shifts and swallows her way out of sleep, brushes with the back of her hand at the damp patch of drool on her cheek. Her ankles, raised on a footstool, come into focus. Swollen. Around her, the dogs are yelping, wanting out. One of them might have done something already in the house, there's that smell again. Frank will go nuts. He hates the dogs and he'd as soon lift one of them with his foot when he's passing as not. She better straighten the place out, not go giving him reasons.

Besides, it's Tuesday.

She hauls herself out of the chair, scattering the coupons and newspapers she forgot were in her lap. Frank hates her coupons. Says he doesn't need food stamps, thank you very much. She gave up explaining the difference long since. Besides, he already knows the difference; he's just being contrary. She keeps cutting the coupons because she can save five or ten dollars a shop, but since Frank drives her to the store, she never gets to use them. She must have ten cookie tins full by now, most all of them out of date.

She puts the dogs out but she's wheezing hard from the exertion. It's the weight that slows her down. She didn't always used to be this heavy. She really should try and reduce— Now where did she put that darn— She finds her inhaler, in the pocket of her muumuu where it should be, takes three short puffs. This darn heat. Tugging the synthetic fabric free where her dress has stuck to her thighs, she shuffles to turn the AC up a notch. That ought to do it. Should be nice and cool in time for the kids' lessons. The kids. A whoosh of well-being washes over her and the heat isn't bothering her nearly as much.

Tuesdays are good. After Paulie Walsh – bless the child, music is for everyone, and he has just so much energy, but he is completely without talent – after Paulie's lesson, it's Kane. And after Kane . . . As usual Judy has no one coming after Kane. She likes to let his time run on as long as possible, whenever his mother will allow it. Every lesson culminates in a tiny struggle, because both of them want Kane to keep playing, but Judy knows the mother can't afford more time and is too proud to let his time run without paying. So much potential. And only six. She will have to give him up soon, pass him on to the Music Institute. She worries that the mother won't be able to afford their enormous fees. She will tell her today that they must work hard and stay late, to make sure he wins one of the scholarship places. She's feeling pleased with this plan, but it saddens her, too.

There's that prickle behind her eyes again, but she can hardly help it. Kane is so much like her Joseph at the same age. Such talent. It was her mother all over again, playing through his fingers. His gift, his wonderful, wonderful gift. At least he never followed his father into the used-car business, at least she can be thankful for that.

Judy moves around slowly, straightening things out. Tuesdays are good. Joseph is in the city Tuesdays. She knows, because she saw him drive by the house one time. She was standing by the window, just looking out at nothing, when she saw his van go straight by, without even slowing down. She could not believe it.

—I could not believe it, she exclaimed to Frank that evening. Straight by, without even slowing down. Without even looking at the house. His own home.

—What's not to believe, Frank said from behind the sports page.

—That he could—

—I know what you mean, Frank said levelly. I just don't know why you are surprised, is all.

—Well . . . Judy was flustered. Frank was right. Joseph never called by. Not unless he really had to. Thanksgiving, Christmas. That was about it.

—Well, I'm going to pick up the phone right now and find out why a son would not call in to his own mother when he's passing by.

But Frank had raised his paper with that slow deliberateness of his, and was no longer listening. No reasonable conclusions could be reached by discussing their son. They each lived with their own private version of disappointment where Joseph was concerned, and there was no overlap.

She moved to the counter and picked up the phone.

—Um . . . Joseph said.

—You know, busy . . . Joseph said.

—Next time . . . Joseph said.

Judy picked him up on it in a flash.

—Next time you're—

—You know, next time, the wholesalers . . .

—So you go to the *wholesalers, every Tuesday*?

She could imagine Frank's bushy eyebrows lifting behind his newspaper. And Joseph had conceded that, yes, every Tuesday. Then he modified it to *most* Tuesdays. Most Tuesdays he was in Chicago at the wholesalers, and yes, he would, one of the days when he wasn't so busy, stop by to see his mother.

—There, Judy put the phone down with a flourish.

—He's not gonna come over, Frank said, without looking up.

But you never know, he just might. She doesn't know when she saw him last. He's just so darn busy. Frank drives out there sometimes. He doesn't go to see his son, he goes to keep an eye on his investment. Well, maybe next time she will surprise them both, take a drive out with him. Soon as the weather cools down a bit. The fall, maybe. It's nice, being in the nature when the leaves are turning. Yes, that's what she's going to do.

She lowers her bulk onto the piano stool, smiling as she imagines herself in the passenger seat of Frank's Cadillac, leaving Chicago behind, heading out on the open road into the heart of Midwest America. She will take that tour of Joseph's farm, try out some of his vegetables. She wonders what might be in season in the fall. Corn? Pumpkin? She will make Mother's pumpkin challah. She can already see herself, taking the hot yeasty loaves out of Joseph's oven. But then she remembers. No challah. Mother is long gone, but Frank is of the same mind as her mother. No Jewish cooking. No Jewish anything. Funny how she can't seem to get it into her head, even after all these years.

She glances at the clock. If Joseph is coming, he'd better hurry, because the children will be here soon. He'd never come after, not if there's any chance Frank might be there. Poor Joseph, having to take a loan from Frank that time. It must have killed him. No, they do not get on. She does not want to think about them, toe to toe, not getting on.

Maybe she will make him pumpkin pie instead when she takes that drive out. They'll sit in Joseph's kitchen, filled with cinnamon smells, and talk. In her mind's ear they are talking in German. But that would never happen, not with Frank around. She wonders if Joseph remembers, when he was little, chatting away to her in the language she was not able to forget, even when Mother insisted. That was when he was still playing piano. When he still chatted to her. The happiest time of her life.

Her fingers have crept onto the keyboard, remembering a jolly little song, one of the very first Joseph learned. He played it by ear when he was hardly more than three. Straight in, starting at an *f*. But then she plays *a-flat*, not the *a* that belongs to the tune. With *b*, *c*, dissonant, melancholic, unfinished.

Yehudit is six. They have been walking for a long time. She is tired, but Mother is even more tired so she carries her own small bag. In it is a piece of hard bread, and the photograph. Then there is a train, then more walking. It seems to be night for a long time, and it is still dark when they reach the end of the road. A wooden bridge is slung across black water to a boat. Mother flinches when the man who is standing there puts out his hand to help her across. He pulls his hand back, says something in a language Yehudit does not understand, and steps a little away. Mother seems very tall and all alone as she walks across. She does not hold the ropes, even though the bridge rocks and sways.

The boat takes a long time. She plays with the other children: Adam, Solomon. She can't remember the other girl's name. They hide all over, even in the Captain's quarters. He is nice to them and smiles a lot, but still he seems sad.

She is American now, Mother tells her, with one of those same, sad smiles. This will be their home, this small apartment with one bedroom, a toilet on the landing. She does not know why Mother cries the day the knock comes on the door and the two American men bring in a piano.

—There ya go, missy, one of them says, mussing Yehudit's hair.

But the piano is not for her, it is for Mother, and she cries when she plays it, probably because she is remembering the pretty dress, the tall handsome man leaning on another big, shiny piano, smiling down at her while she played: the people in the photograph.

Mother was sad the day Yehudit came home from school crying because everyone was speaking in English and she did not understand what they were saying.

—You will, Yehudit. In time you will understand.

She said it like *You-dith*. Except at school they said *Ju-dith*. The teacher even spelled it wrong in the roll book.

She made some friends after a while. *Wait up, Jude*, they called, rushing to link arms on the way to school, the way girls do. Only, Mother heard, *Wait up, Jew*. Judith tried to explain but it didn't matter. From then on, Mother stopped observing the holiday and reading the Torah, and Yehudit became Judy. Mother looked sad again when she heard Judy's friends call her.

Later, when Judy got in from school, Mother was tired as well as sad. She had to cut back her hours at the store where she worked, but before long she was too tired even for that. When she was too ill to work anymore, Judy said goodbye to high school and her friends and stayed home to look after her. Even when she had done everything – helped her to swallow her pills, cleaned her up, fixed her pillows – she could tell that Mother was still in pain. She didn't say anything, but Judy could see it in her eyes. Then, when she could not take the pain away with pills or comfortable pillows, Judy played piano. Mother had been a patient teacher, and Judy a good, though not gifted, pupil, and as she stroked the keys into melodies from her mother's past a temporary peace crept into the apartment, enveloping them both.

When there was no more money, sixteen-year-old Judy did not know where to turn. The neighbour across the hall was good to them, but she did not have much herself. Go to Maxwell Street, she told Judy. There, old man Rosenberg would give her cash for anything she had to sell. Judy went. She put her head down and wove her way through the pandemonium of upturned boxes and crates heaving with wares; the cacophony of accents – German, Irish, Italian, and plenty more she did not recognise – peddling lamps, television sets, bikes, strange-smelling clothes, all competing with the sliding blue notes of harmonicas and guitars. The pullers called to her, tugged on her sleeve, tried to entice her in to the stores. She drew her coat more tightly around her and hurried on until she found it: *Rosenbergs Jewelry*.

He was about a hundred, but he was the one sitting her down and getting her water to drink.

—There, he said in Hebrew. You feel better, eh?

57

Judy nodded, still feeling weak, not trusting herself to speak, in any language.

—You are Laila's girl? he asked gently.

Judy nodded again.

—She is not well, I hear.

She shook her head.

—Laila, Laila, they took all her strength from her.

Judy did not know what he meant, but the old man was talking more to himself than to her.

—Terrible, terrible, he was saying. Terrible times. All the poor little children. Poor Laila. Poor Jacob.

Then he seemed to remember again that she was there.

—I knew your grandfather, he said softly, and he counted out far too many dollars in exchange for her mother's watch.

When there was nothing else, Judy sold the piano, and when her mother begged with her eyes for some music, Judy could only stare at her hands where they sat palm up in her lap, her fingers as useless as the flailing legs of an upturned beetle.

When her mother died, Mr Grube the store owner took pity on her and gave Mother's old job to Judy, though she knew nothing at all about counting and measuring, and she was too quiet to be any good with the customers. But she turned up in good time every day with her face well-scrubbed and her hair in a tidy braid, ready and willing to do her best.

When a certain Frank Martello started coming in too often, Mr Grube winked and told her she'd want to look out for those Italians. After that, Judy blushed every time he came in. She fumbled his change and stammered answers to his questions, so it came as a complete surprise when he leaned his elbow on the counter and asked her how she'd like to come work for him, in a nice office job. Mr Grube joined in from the store-room.

—You going to pay her well, eh?

—I'll double her wages, Frank replied, quick as a shot, with a wink to Judy, who blushed to the soles of her feet.

—Then get outta here fast as your feet can carry you, Judy, Mr Grube said.

Frank was as good as his word. He gave her such an easy job that she wondered if he thought she was an idiot, but she was happy to hide away in the quiet office behind his own, at the back of the lot. Every day he came in for a chat, to put her at her ease. He was such a talker. That was why he was so good at selling cars. He talked her into filling in at reception before long, and when she protested that she couldn't possibly, looking down at her faded skirt and well-washed sweater, he took her by the two hands and danced her out of the office and into one of the fancy sporty cars, the best in the showroom.

—Then we're going downtown, pretty lady.

He brought her to State Street, to the famous Marshall Field's.

—Pick out whatever you want, Frank said grandly.

Judy had never set foot inside the door of Marshall Field's before. The doorman intimidated her, the perfumes overwhelmed her, and she hardly dared to lift her eyes.

When Frank noticed, he grabbed a saleswoman by the arm.

—My girl here could use a little help finding something nice.

That was the first day he called her his girl. Frank could be kind back then. He bought her a caramel twinset and a mustard dirndl skirt and a box of Frango mints.

After they got married, Frank didn't like her working in the lot any more.

—What do you want, hanging around those guys all day? he asked, and she didn't have an answer to that. She didn't have answers to many of the questions husbands ask because she had never heard them answered; she did not remember her father and mother together, only in the photograph. She spent her days in their new home on the South Side. She was lonesome, but she told herself they would soon fill those empty bedrooms.

The bedrooms stayed empty, and Judy found it

harder to count her blessings every day. Living with Mother had been like living with a shadow, moving silently about, getting everything done with the least amount of fuss. Frank was the opposite. He never talked when he could shout, he left doors open, and the television was on from the time he got up in the morning, and again from the moment he got home, with the volume up high.

Sometimes she didn't know she was crying, and when he'd ask her what in tarnation was the matter she'd have to put a hand to her cheek and feel it wet to realise. When he looked into her dark eyes she could see his incomprehension, but she also knew that he did not want to understand what he saw in there. He did not want to know what her dark eyes had seen, and he covered his fear with impatience, then with anger, so the house swung between oppressive silences and frustrated outbursts, frequently followed by a slamming door, then silence again.

—What? Frank asked her when he came back from whatever bar he'd gone to. What do you want from me?

He sat down heavily onto their bed, where she lay with her back to him, her face pressed into her damp pillow.

—What do you want, Judy? he asked, more gently.
She whispered it, so he didn't hear at first.
—Ya what?
She lifted her head so he could hear better.
—A piano.

Frank liked people to know he could afford the best.
He pulled the blankets off with a flourish.

—What do you think, Judy? Think this'll make
her happy, boys? he asked the delivery men, his audience. They were standing back, two Irishmen, letting
him have his moment, probably hoping for a tip.
What do you say we get her to give us a tune? What
about one of Johnny Ace's. Come on, Baby. *Never
Let Me Go*. Can't have these boys saying you weren't
worth the top of the range.

Judy had never played for anyone except her
mother before and she could feel her hands trembling.
She moved to the piano, then looked around her
vaguely.

—A stool . . . ?

Frank's look turned dark, until he spotted the
smaller object by the door. Then he was all smiles
again.

—A stool, boys. Give the lady a stool.

The stool was unveiled and placed behind her.

Judy knew the melody; Frank was fond of playing

it in his car at full volume. She brought her fingers to the smooth ivory, releasing a single pure note with only the lightest of touches, and another. Then another, all in minor thirds. There was something in the resonance that fixed them all in the stillness, made even Frank shut up. Then, when the last whisper of the chord died away, Judy's right hand picked out the melody they wanted to hear, and her left hand joined in with the simple runs the song required. Frank accompanied her loudly, off-key.

On their way down the front steps, after pocketing a five-dollar bill, one of the movers said under his breath, *feckin' eejit*, and something about shooting himself. Judy didn't find out until later that they were talking about the singer, Johnny Ace, who had accidentally shot himself with a loaded gun.

The house became filled with the music Mother had taught her. Frank complained that it always sounded sad, but she couldn't help it, the melancholy seemed to go further back than she did, maybe back to her mother, growing up in a place Judy didn't know, and couldn't imagine. Or couldn't remember. But it was what she heard resonating in her ear. She had to remember to wipe the tears away before Frank came home. Though she wasn't unhappy, he wouldn't understand.

Then, at last, Joseph came. Judy liked to think she had played him into being. He was dark-eyed and dark-skinned, and Frank said he was the image of the Napoli Paolini's on his mother's side, but Judy knew he was of her. As soon as he could reach the keys, he played. At two or three he copied what she showed him, her shadow treble, her shadow bass.

By the time he was six, Joseph could play Mahler as well as small hands would allow. Though he didn't understand the music, the feeling of angst, seeping from the fingers of his small son, made Frank frown. Judy taught Joseph to play Debussy's *Feuilles Mortes* and Ravel's dreamy, melancholic *Oiseaux Tristes* instead. Frank still grumbled, not understanding, but he left them alone.

The day before Joseph's seventh birthday they were doing finger exercises, Joseph speeding up and down the keyboard in finger-perfect semitones. Every note was a dart in Judy's flesh, because she was preparing Joseph for the Music Institute entrance exams; he was too good for her. They had already come out to hear him play, the President of the Institute himself, and another woman. They had stopped in the porch – Judy saw them through the window – listening to Joseph practicing. They shook their heads, and looked at each other, and nodded their heads. This was all

64

before they even pressed the bell. The exam was a formality, they said when they were leaving.

Up and down the keyboard, four octaves, Joseph's tongue protruded slightly in concentration. Neither of them saw it coming: the little hands, side-swiped off the keys, the lid slammed down. Frank looked at them while the wood resounded in their ears, daring them. In his hand he held a mitt and a ball and a bat.

—That stuff's for little kids, Joey. Little kids and sissies. It's Little League from now on. Time to forget about all that music.

Judy has a surprise planned. Young Kane will make a start on the Symphony No. 5 piano transcription, Mahler. Half-German, that's what his mother said when they first came. German, Austrian, it was close enough. The mother was Japanese, and she had sought Judy out having heard of her reputation from Kane's school. Kane stood beside her, serious and quiet, while Judy explained to his mother, who wanted him to learn the Suzuki method, that she could only teach the method she had learned from her mother. It didn't have a name, she said.

Her fingers are giddy with anticipation, but before she can tease the keys with the opening bars the doorbell rings. Paulie Walsh. As she goes to let the child in she sets aside the familiar, dull disappointment that precedes the child's lesson every Tuesday – because another week has passed that Joseph didn't come – and she fills the vacant place with enough justifications to make it right.

Paulie is red haired and freckled and as always he looks, with his hair sticking out and his clothing all askew, as if he just fell out of a tree. He makes Judy think of that show Joseph used to watch, *Leave it to Beaver*.

—How are you, Paulie? Judy asks, with a wave to Paulie's mother, who is waiting in the car.

—Ya know, Mrs M., same ol' same ol'.

Judy laughs.

—I hope not, she says. You promised you would practise this week.

—Yes, Mrs Martello, Paulie says, his step losing some of its bounce.

Judy lets him have a go at his piece, a simple little tune he's been torturing for months now, and as expected, it doesn't go well.

—Let's try this, she says. We'll sing it. I'll sing first – *lala lala laaa* – now you—

—La la la la la, Paulie intones miserably.

—*Lala lala laaa*? Judy tries again.

—La la la la la.

Judy inhales, then slowly exhales. She's getting too old for this. If it wasn't for Kane—

—Clapping, she says. We'll try clapping out the music, Paulie. It's all about rhythm. Let's go.

But the clapping is a failure too. Judy glances at the clock. Too soon to let him out to his mother. She will have to have a chat with her one of these days.

The piece is illustrated with lambs, frolicking on a hillside.

—I know, Judy says. Colour. We will colour the picture.

She lumbers to the sideboard to rummage for materials. Paulie gives her a cynical look, which changes to resignation when he, too, glances at the clock. To its too slow, metronomic increments, Paulie scratches away at the lambs with a crayon.

—Thanks, Mrs M., Paulie calls, as he bounds down the steps.

—Practise, Paulie, Judy says as she waves him off.

She is already distracted, looking up and down the road to see if there is any sign of Kane. His mother usually walks with him from Grand and Milwaukee Station. Usually, they are there, waiting on the steps. They are never late.

She goes back inside eventually, not wanting the neighbours to witness her anxious waiting. She's wheezing again. Her inhaler— Where is it—? Ah. She takes three puffs. She waits. She looks at the photograph on the piano, her beautiful mother looking at her father looking back at her as she plays. The only sounds in the front room come from the second hand of the clock, pressing relentlessly forward into the second half of Kane's lesson, and the far-away whine of her own inhalations.

Áine

Áine is sitting on the empty trestle table watching Joe load the van. The crowds have gone, arms full of preserves and flowers and dried gourds and organic vegetables, home to their Saturday evenings. She wonders how Daisy spent hers at Conor's. If she was at home, instead of playing at farmers' market, they'd probably have had pizza and a treat, and watched the Big Big Movie together. She'd be asleep by now, though – she takes out her phone to check – six hours ahead.

All around them, traders are packing away their stalls, calling to each other across the clatter of the clean-up.

—Busy enough for ya, Ty?

—Uh huh.

—Whole season like that, we'll be doin' OK.

—That's for sure.

Áine likes the way the voices feel far away, that end of workday feeling, when everyone's too tired to have an agenda, when there's a camaraderie, workers united in wanting to get home. She held her own today with that couple with the basils, if she says so herself. She's earned a nice glass of wine. God, her legs are throbbing from all the standing.

Joe lifts a stack of boxes, bending properly at the knees. He has a nice arse from all that honest-to-god farming. He glances over.

—You gonna lend a hand or what?

Her pause is barely perceptible, but she has already figured out that he is a perceptive kind of guy. She slides down and picks up an emptied strawberry tray.

—Busy today, she says brightly.

—Mm hm.

—Any plans for this evening?

It'd be nice to see those lakes she's heard about, go for a drive. She's thinking picnic, long grass, a nice chilled chardonnay, sun on their bodies. After all, she only has a few days left. The week is flying by.

He raises his eyebrows and shakes his head at the kind of farmer she's not, never mind that he's only been farming a few years himself, as far as she's been able to figure out.

—Farm work's never finished, Áine.

Farm work's never finished, Áine, she mimics in her head.

She was warned, in fairness. He was nothing if not explicit in his many, long emails, and even longer calls on Skype. *Hard worker, companion . . .*

Not internet dating, Jesus, she wasn't that desperate. But when Maeve in the office mentioned that her cousin had been a wwoofer on this farm in Illinois . . .

—A what?

—World Wide Opportunities on Organic Farms, Maeve spelled it out for her. Sort of volunteering, learning a new trade . . . Exploitation, if you ask me, but no one does . . .

. . . and that the farmer guy wasn't half bad, something switched on in her. A notion, her mother would call it.

Conor had already been gone two years, and she missed him only in the guilt-shaped package their traditional wedding and semi-d mortgage had promised. They met at work, in the lift; he was two floors down. When she thought about it afterwards, it was incredibly smug of both of them to presume the other wanted what they wanted themselves. Because, as it turned out, Áine hadn't a clue what she wanted.

Five years after she proudly filled her new kitchen presses with the wedding Denby and the Nicholas Mosse, she still hadn't figured it out. But there was one thing that she knew she wanted by then, she told Conor. She wanted a divorce.

She waited two full weeks for her wwoofer notion to fizzle out, and when it didn't she finally brought it up with Maeve.

—Em. How's your cousin getting on – Rachel, isn't it?

—Grand.

Maeve turned back to her computer.

—The . . . em . . . wwoofer thing, it went well?

—Said it was a good experience anyway. Broadened her horizons and that. Knuckling down now, though. She's heading into her finals this semester.

Back to her spreadsheet. She clacked away on her keyboard for a few minutes before the penny dropped at last.

—Surely you're not thinking . . . You mean . . . You?

—Well, why not . . .

—Well, it's the kind of thing . . . I mean, Rachel's a student. It was a temporary visa thing, you know, once of those J1s. You're . . . And what about work? And Daisy?

Then she laughed – Áine must be joking – and went back to work.

When Maeve and Robbie's anniversary rolled around the following week, Maeve did a big dinner, surrounding herself with friends and family. Áine got her mother to pick Daisy up and went straight from work to help out. As luck would have it, Rachel was there too, offering little bite-sized things around on trays, but Áine couldn't bring herself to ask about the farm. If Maeve found the idea ludicrous – a thirty-something, mother-of-one, civil servant going off to some farm to find herself – twenty-year-old Rachel was sure to drop her tray of canapés laughing. She pasted a smile on her face and wandered around nodding at the half familiar faces.

When Robbie waylaid her, put a drink in her hand, introduced her to a middle-aged man, patted her on the back, and left, it didn't take genius to figure out that she was being set up. Again. Maeve and Robbie seemed to have decided that she had been on her own long enough, and for the past six months they'd been digging up single men, usually in insurance and banking, always with long, sad faces, and longer, sadder stories. Hadn't they learned anything at all from her divorce from Conor? Sometimes she wondered if they saw her singledom as some sort of threat. But at least they were motivated, which was more than she could say for herself.

This one was another of Robbie's colleagues, big, divorced, and a father of four. Through aperitifs and into the starter, they hedged around the obvious question. Had he asked, she was likely to have mumbled something about irreconcilable differences, or growing apart, whereas what she wanted to blurt was, *boredom. I was dying of boredom!*

Though of course the question wasn't asked. No questions were asked. Instead, he talked about Robbie, and rugby, his four boys, and himself. Finally her bladder got the better of her inertia.

—Jesus, get me out of here, she pleaded to Rachel, who'd taken herself to the kitchen and substituted her tray for a very full glass of red.

Rachel laughed and filled a glass for Áine.

—You look like you need it.

They sipped their wine in the relative peace of the kitchen, listening to the drone of the party in the next room, punctuated every so often with overloud guffaws from the men and high-pitched shrieks from the women. It made Áine feel exhausted.

—Maeve said you were interested in the Illinois thing I did.

74

Áine formed a surprised-sounding *Illinois?* in her mouth, to look like she didn't know what Rachel was talking about, but a louder voice from inside her thought differently, and she heard herself say that, yes, it sounded like a wonderful experience, and would Rachel mind passing on a contact address? she'd be interested in finding out more. She felt her face burning as she spoke, and hoped it looked as if she was flushed from the wine, but Rachel didn't seem to notice anything.

—Sure. What's your number? I'll text it. Word to the wise, she added when Áine's phone beeped and the contact was transferred. Joe's a fine thing, but the place is a tip.

Áine grinned and shrugged and blushed her confusion, but Rachel just smiled enigmatically and went back to her wine.

Daisy's fifth birthday was a few weeks later. When the last of the high-pitched kids left with the last of their chattering mothers, and Daisy's predictable sugar-crash tantrum had cried itself out into sleep, Áine mopped the drink-sticky floor and wiped the last granite surface dry and put on the dishwasher. Then she sat down for the first time all day. The remote was on top of the telly, but she hadn't the energy to get it, so she sat in the silent room in front of the black screen. She could see herself reflected, her head slumped, her hair flattened. Even if she had been in full technicolour she knew she would be washed out to shadow greys. She forced herself not to move, to sit there with herself. Compared to the fluffy-haired, iPhone-busy young woman she'd spotted perched in the passenger seat of Conor's Yaris while he dashed in to give Daisy her present, she was a non-event. That was the word. That was her. Her whole life was a long, predictable non-event: school, civil service exams, work. Conor. It was no wonder Maeve and Robbie found the kinds of men they found for her. They were hardly going to pair someone like her up with a fire-eating limbo-dancer they'd picked up on Grafton Street. Not that they would ever stop to talk to someone so exotic and unpredictable.

The dishwasher shifted from a white hum into full-on whooshing and whirring, and she was relieved because it meant the room wasn't silent any more.

That was the moment, when a dishwasher was company, when she knew something had to be done. That was when she remembered the wilfully forgotten contact Rachel had sent to her phone.

First, she couldn't find her phone. She ended up tipping the entire contents of her oversized bag onto the counter before locating it among the chaos.

Then she couldn't find the message. She hoped it wasn't an omen, telling her not to be making ridiculous mistakes. But a third scroll through yielded what she was looking for: *joethefarmer@hotmail.com*. She tried to imagine her father, before he died, describing himself as *the farmer*, but since she couldn't imagine him on email in the first place, she gave up.

Joethefarmer, here goes nothing.

She went into the spare room, which doubled as office and general dumping ground. The old PC was buried under a pile of clothes Daisy had grown out of and which were waiting for a charity shop run. She switched it on and waited for it to boot up. As usual there was nothing in her email account but spam; anyone who wanted her knew to contact her at work. She opened a new mail and typed it in. *joethefarmer@*, then deleted it immediately. What if she hit *Send* by accident before she had phrased herself properly? She moved the cursor to the body of the email. *Dear Joe.* But was he a potential employer? Should he be *Dear Sir*? She discarded that idea. joethefarmer was no *Sir*. Maybe she should go with casual, act like she was in charge, like she might or might not consider . . .

Hi Joe, My name is Áine. I got your address from Rachel, who was a WWOOFer there last summer. It was a start. She'd keep it short and sweet. *I'm interested in finding out more about your farm, and what*

77

being a WWOOFer entails. Yours . . . She sent it
before she could think about it, turned off the
computer, and went to bed.

She didn't get a chance to check the computer until
she got home from work, but the email she got back
had been sent within minutes of hers, and although
it read like a standard response to a query, it was a
thrill to see it there, nestled among the ads for Viagra
and penis extensions. His was the only real email
there. All about the farm, tomatoes and peppers,
hoophouses and tomatillos. The unfamiliar words
alone were exciting. Wwoofers did everything, by all
accounts, and received, in return, *a stipend*. Pocket
money. Áine smiled at the idea. But she liked the
flow of his email. There was something there, intel-
ligence, and something else. *Sounds great*, she typed
fast. *I'm not much of a farmer but . . .*

This time she left the computer on while she
poured herself a glass of Chianti, and by the time
she got back, his reply was there. *I can tell you have
the right kind of attitude. You'll learn.* He was
flattering her, and talking as if it was a foregone
conclusion that she'd go out there wwoofing, if that
was a word. She typed words to this effect, stopping
only to sip at her wine. The exchange went back and
forth until after midnight and three glasses of wine,

and it was she who, reluctantly, closed the exchange, thinking of work in the morning.

The next day, she couldn't wait to get home. He asked if she would send a photo of herself, and, by way of encouragement, sent one of himself. He was standing in a field, holding up a bunch of deformed-looking purple tomatoes, shirtless. Was this normal protocol for hiring a wwoofer? He was a fine thing, exactly as Rachel had reported. Dark hair, nice body, hairy but not too hairy, though she wasn't mad about the beard. She sent the only photo she had on the computer, a not very flattering one from a work-do, and she was vaguely insulted when he passed no comment on it either way.

They alternated between a back-and-forth volley of short, witty chat when they were online at the same time, and long, intense analyses of their respective situations when they were at their computers alone. It seemed, in the winter at least, that he was alone on the farm, and not inclined to seek out company. She was surrounded by people all day, and she had Daisy, but the evenings and the nights, she typed with nervous fingers, were lonely. She hit *Send* and was immediately sorry, her *I'm in control here* persona erased in a line. She needn't have worried. He was back in under a minute. *You're lonely, I'm lonely. We should Skype.*

She liked that he could type fast. So many men

at work who used computers all day kept stabbing away with two fingers rather than submit to beginner-typist status (Conor was one of them). And she liked the anonymity of writing. She could half-make herself up as she went. Skype was another story, though. She was nervous of the phone. Phones were intrusive. One half of a conversation with this stranger would reverberate around the walls of her home, her and Daisy's home. And Skype . . . But, she had to admit, the emails had exhausted them-selves. *Ok*, she typed.

She didn't get around to it for a couple of days. There were parent-teacher meetings on at Daisy's school, then it was work's monthly movie night: *I Love You Phillip Morris*. Maura, who was in charge of Ents and had booked the tickets, was mortified. She was expecting their usual romcom. Still, anything with Ewan McGregor was nice to look at.

Joe was annoyed. She'd disappeared, he said. He didn't know if she was going to come back. He'd missed her. She was the only one he wanted to talk to. She considered his email for a while. This was a bit too intense, from someone she barely knew. But he was exciting, and nothing like Robbie's friend, whose name she hadn't bothered to remember, or any of the selection of men Maeve had produced. Not to mention that Áine hadn't managed to produce a single one herself. That clinched it. *Skype*, she typed in, hoping it wasn't hard to set up. Conor was the one who used to do that sort of thing.

Joe talked enough for both of them. He wasn't interested in Daisy's progress at school, it turned out, or Phillip Morris and poor Maura's mistake. That was OK; she shouldn't expect him to be, she reasoned. Instead, he talked fast and without pause, mostly about his ideas for the farm, how he was going to rotate the onions with vetch, whatever that was, how he could use another hoophouse to start seeds. She found herself tuning out from time to time.

—Why not come and check it out for yourself? he dropped in, mid-spiel. So casual she nearly missed it. They'd only been in contact a couple of weeks and he was already inviting her to *check it out*.

—Are you sure it's not *me* you want to check out? she asked, with a lifted eyebrow.

But his screen had frozen, he said, and he didn't catch what she'd said. Skype wasn't all it was cracked up to be, Áine decided. Whatever his motives, it didn't seem to bother him that it involved a transatlantic flight, or that she had work and Daisy to consider. Men. She'd go if it suited her.

Maeve reacted the way Áine expected her to react. This was a big step. What about Daisy? Had she worked up enough leave? Was she sure she was doing the right thing? Áine had her answers ready: only a week . . . Rachel's already been there . . . Daisy will go to Conor, he's always looking for more time with her. But Maeve's frowning concern resonated with the undisguised pity she'd heard behind Conor's mild-toned *What are you playing at, Áine?* and a gash opened up in her, as raw as a piece of liver fresh from the butcher.

—I am going, Maeve, so I don't go insane.

She had to take herself off to the Ladies so she wouldn't have to look at the expression on Maeve's face.

By five o'clock, Maeve had rallied.

—A week away will do you good. Would you get a bit of sun there this time of year, do you think?

Relief flooded through Áine as she hugged her friend.

She went into a frenzy of passports and tickets, and waxing and tweezing, and six weeks later Daisy went to Conor and Áine went to Chicago.

She didn't know what to expect at O'Hare, but between nerves and jetlag, she was a mess. In the restroom, she fingered Moroccan oil through her newly highlighted hair, powdered away any last blemishes, topped up her lippie, and walked out. In O'Hare you were straight into arrivals, no buffer zone, and here she was, face to face with Joe. They hugged awkwardly and he didn't offer to carry her bag out to his car. His dirty, litter-strewn car. She regretted her white 7s. Besides, it was too hot for jeans, and she could see that he thought so too. He was in khaki shorts, showing off muscular brown calves. She'd got it all wrong.

—Never mind, he said, though she hadn't actually said anything. We'll soon get you changed out of those.

This only heightened her anxiety. The new, adventurous side of Áine was barely formed, and it shrank away now in this stranger's car, leaving in its place visions of rape and bondage in what sounded like an Addams Family house. When he pulled up the driveway she saw that she wasn't far off. What would once have been a charming, colonial-style house, with a big porch running all along one side, hadn't seen a lick of paint in fifty years and, worryingly, seemed to sag in places.

He didn't bring her in right away. Instead, he took her on a whirlwind tour of his farm. There were sheds called nurseries, where tiny herbs grew in trays under heat lamps, and processing houses, where some of the produce was made into preserves. Áine nodded *Hello* to the man setting glass jars out on a worktop.

—Carlos, Joe told her, before moving her impatiently on to the next attraction. He did not tell Carlos her name.

He was talking like an auctioneer the whole time, even worse than on the phone. She was only able to take in bits with the tiredness. She had been up at four to get to the airport, and he hadn't as much as offered her a glass of water. It was fascinating all the same, the stages of the plants, the different crops she knew nothing about, the hoophouses, which turned out to be plastic greenhouses – *polytunnels* at home – filled with the tangy, invigorating smell of the young tomato plants.

—These'll be heaving with heirlooms when you guys come back, Joe commented.

All through the asparagus and the raspberries, and his bitter commentary about the tall green corn that bordered his farm and threatened it with sprays and fertilisers, she was bouncing that one around in her mind.

When he could no longer avoid it, it seemed to her, he brought her inside the house. She had never seen anything like it. There were smells of must, and cats or dogs or . . . She didn't want to think what. Maybe she should have paid more attention to Rachel's warning. He had the grace to be a little bit sheepish.

—The winter . . . he said.

—Needs work, he said.

—Before you guys come back in the summer, he said.

As if she would ever bring Daisy to a dump like this.

84

He took her hand, their first touch since the airport, and brought her upstairs. It was a little better up here. The bedroom was tidy, if not exactly clean. He put his hands onto her hips and drew her into a long, exploratory kiss. Her body, untouched by man for over two years, gave in long before her mind had intended to. She didn't know if it was the long drought, or if he was the hottest lover since Rasputin, but when she lay back after, onto the rough wool blanket, she'd never felt as, well, *serviced*, in her whole life.

He was gone to smoke, he'd said. She'd smiled at the cliché, but when he hadn't come back after ages, she got up to find him. He was half-asleep in his den – a tiny, overheated room, filled with his recliner chair and the TV, which he had on with the sound down. There was a strong, pungent smell.

— 'S up? he asked. Áine, he added, as if reminding himself.

—Just wondered where you'd got to, she said, aiming to sound sweet.

He looked at her for a moment, then patted the arm of his chair.

—Here. Let me roll you one.

The smell. She was an eejit. It wasn't like he'd kept his dope smoking secret. He talked about it non-stop, mostly about how he smoked too much in winter and planned to cut back. She hadn't wanted to think about it. Littered around him were cigarette papers, a bag of dried leaf stuff, a lighter; and his hands were moving deftly, combining them quickly into a fat joint, which he held out to her. She wondered how Maeve would react, or Conor. *What are you playing at, Áine?* She took it between her thumb and index finger gingerly, as if it might explode if she didn't handle with care. Joe laughed.

—You're not a smoker, are you? Here, let me . . .

He took the joint and lit it. —Sstheee, he sucked a little smoke in and held it. Then another, and another, until his chest was puffed and his gaze had moved somewhere inwards. Still holding his breath, he passed it to her. Determined to try something new, she inhaled. Too much.

—Take it easy, he laughed through his exhalation. He patted her on the back and she felt like part of something. There. Better? Try again, just a little this time, huh?

She was more careful, taking just a tiny suck. He held up his free hand to high-five her – something else new.

—Way to go, Áine.

She took another small drag. She was getting the hang of this. Soon she was giggling at everything he said, everything she said herself. Drugs weren't as bad as she'd been led to believe.

She spent her first night with Joe having sometimes

86

languorous, sometimes abandoned sex, on his recliner, against the wall, against the window, on the filthy floor. Hours of climbing onto and over each other, of staying still, of falling into each other again. Never had she felt so uninhibited.

When she woke she was naked, covered in patches of ash and dirt and she didn't like to think what, alone on top of his bed. She brushed off the bed cover and went to take a shower. As she passed the door, she spotted him in his den, fully dressed, mouth open, snoring in his recliner.

Which was where he slept the next two nights as well.

They've had sex once since. This morning, while they were getting the produce ready for the market, he led her into the hoophouse where he grabbed her into a hard kiss, pulling off her top as he pressed her in among the tomato plants. She was half-aware that Carlos must have been somewhere around, and that guy Rick, the mature student who did the other market, could turn up at any minute, but the heady scent from the young leaves, and the pure smell of lust, overcame her inhibitions, and it was just as electrifying as before. One thing's for sure, a tomato will never smell the same again.

She's going to have to figure out how to get him to

sleep in his own bed, though. It's been too long since she's woken up beside a man. She'll be sorry when she has to go home, and she's not ready to admit it, but seeds of possibility are sending up tiny shoots into her brain. *When you guys come back in the summer . . .*

She straightens up her tired back, then reluctantly picks up some more empties and takes the lot to the van. Out of the corner of her eye, a woman, coming in their direction, appears to stop dead when she spots Joe. Then, seeing Áine watching, she collects herself and continues towards them.

—I think someone's looking for you, Áine tells Joe.

Joe looks up, then quickly away, but he's too late.

—It *is* you, the woman is saying. I *thought* it was you from way over there. Nice *beard*, Joe.

She's too perky for Áine's liking. She's also lying; she very nearly turned and went the other way when she saw him. And Áine can tell that she doesn't really like the beard. Very *American*, with her golden skin and perfect teeth. Still, she seems friendly. Áine, half in, half out of the van, prepares a smile for her introduction. After all, she'll have to meet his friends sooner or later, especially if . . .

—Hey, Joe says. He does not sound excited to see her. How are you, Vicky?

He takes a few steps away and starts to deconstruct the canopy.

88

—Great. It's been *ages*, she says.

Joe doesn't say anything, starts telescoping metal poles into each other. The woman, Vicky, looks back to where Áine is still stuck, mid-step, on the van. They are both waiting, both embarrassed, yet both seem to want to cover for him. Why? Why not let him look as rude as he is. She climbs down and sticks out her hand.

—Hi, I'm Áine. I'm Joe's . . .

The girl spots the awkward moment straight away.

—Vicky Delorente. We were at school together.

School here means college. Áine is confused.

—Farming?

But now she vaguely remembers him saying something about geology. He does seem to know loads about rocks and soil and stuff. Vicky laughs.

—I wouldn't make much of a farmer.

It's clear she's curious about what kind of a farmer Áine is, and Áine, naturally, is wondering who exactly Vicky is. Joe looks like he wishes she would just disappear. Or that he could. He hasn't stopped twisting and stacking and folding since Vicky got here. He's running out of apparatus to look busy with.

—I'm a teacher, she explains.

—A teacher?

Áine is even more confused now. Joe, a teacher? He never said.

89

Joe chooses this moment to participate.

—You ladies finished . . . ? We have to get going. We're super late. Good to see you again, Vicky. Come on, Áine.

He walks around to the driver's side and climbs in, leaving Áine no option but to follow. Vicky smiles and shrugs, like she's used to him, which makes Áine uncomfortable. But Vicky's smile is open and warm when she says *Nice meeting you.*

—Maybe see you again sometime, Áine concedes, turning towards the van.

—Is that an Irish accent?

—Yep.

—*From* Ireland?

Áine climbs in, with a glance to Joe. She doesn't know whether to be embarrassed or pleased.

—All the way.

—My boyfriend's Irish, Vicky says. You should come down to the Blarney Stone some Friday. It's an Irish bar – but I guess you know that. She laughs. They have really good music.

Joe starts up the engine with a loud rev. He looks like he'd sooner drive over Vicky than let her continue talking, let alone go to this Irish bar.

—To be honest, I'm trying to get away from Ireland at the moment, Áine says, laughing, as Joe starts to pull out. She pulls the door shut, but at some level it's a comfort to know there's a perky Vicky Delorente and an *Irish boyfriend* tucked away in a Blarney Stone somewhere in the city. For emergencies. But thanks, she calls back out the open window.

—So who was that? she asks when they get out into traffic.

Joe is tapping his fingers to the Grateful Dead. She has to ask again.

—She said. Vicky. Vicky Delorente. Good Italian name.

—Like yours.

She turns to examine him. He has the same brown eyes Vicky had. The same dark complexion. An Italian nose. He's Italian all right. And not that she's an expert in these things, but she thinks she can see something else too. His mother's side of the family, maybe. Joe said she was German.

He still hasn't answered her.

—So, who is Vicky Delorente when she's at home?

—Just some girl from college.

—But she's a teacher.

—. . . one-two-three, four-five-six, seven-eight-nine, ten-eleven, one-two-three. 11/12 time, Joe says, without taking his eyes off the road. He's talking about the music. 11/12? She finds herself counting now too . . . seven-eight-nine, ten-eleven, one . . .

—You're right. I did piano for years as a child. I never practised though. Did you do music when you were training to be a . . . a teacher, was it?

Joe snaps the CD player off.

—You want my résumé, Áine? Here it is: Yes. I used to play piano, a long time ago. I also studied geography. Madison. After which I went for my teaching credential, where I met Vicky Delorente. I dropped out. Vicky Delorente presumably did not, and in all likelihood is currently teaching grade school somewhere in the greater Chicago area. Any more questions?

She wants to know why he's so angry. Why he didn't want to introduce her to Vicky. She's supposed to be here to get to know him, isn't she? But when she turns to him with her reprimand on her lips, there's something about the set of his jaw, the fullness of his lips, a quality that she can't name, that stops her. She's sorry now that she didn't just keep her mouth shut and let him tell her in his own time.

They drive out of the city, where industrial parks give way to trees and corn. He relents, put the music back on, reaches under the seat and takes out a beer. He pulls the ring and takes a swig, then hands it to her as an afterthought. She's more of a wine girl, but she takes a drink. Because why come all this way, on this adventure, just to do what she always does.

St. Pauli Girl, the can says, the *Girl* in question bursting out of her *Fraulein* outfit. It's weak and warm and bitter-sweet.

—That's it, Joe says, sweeping an arm across the windscreen. American farming in all its grandeur.

There are fields of green all around. It's nice enough. Áine doesn't know what he means.

—Corn. Lots and lots of corn. For cattle, mostly. And here . . . the soy. Corn and soy. Soy and corn. To feed cattle, to make burgers, to make Midwesterners fatter.

Áine laughs. But he's not joking.

—It's not funny. Americans don't know how to eat any more. And they don't know how to farm any more.

—No, she agrees, pulling back the smile.

He is a serious one. Passionate. About the farm. About her, when he wants to be. Wasn't that what she wanted? Yet here she is, nearly halfway into her so-called reconnaissance, and she still doesn't know what to make of him.

As if he can read her thoughts, her doubts, he takes her hand and rests it on his thigh, sending a tingle through her.

—You hungry? he asks. But he doesn't wait for her answer. He's super hungry, he says. He knows a great place. Nothing fancy, but great food. Really hits the spot.

She is hungry, now that he's brought it up. And he's offering to take her out, which is a nice change.

He pulls up at a gas station.

—Wait here, he says. He jumps out, leaving the engine running.

Through the window of the shop Áine can see him carefully selecting hot dogs from a rotisserie.

Summer 2010

Vicky

She's been turning it over in her mind for weeks and she's pretty sure she's ready. She decided last night. Sure, she'd had a couple of glasses of chardonnay with Susie at the bar, and it's hard to gauge how much that clouds your judgement. Still, she's nearly sure. At any rate, she spent more time than usual getting dressed. Not that John will notice.

When she was drying her hair she saw that there were more greys coming through the dark. She half-closed her eyes until she could see herself in the mirror as if she was looking at someone else. Not too bad, in a squint. Unfortunately, John is not short-sighted, so what he looks at is a less than supple face, heavy hips, and all those greys. Fortunately, what he *thinks* he sees is an attractive woman in her thirties – for another three weeks at least – with a great ass. She twists her lower half so she can appraise her behind, currently poured into her best jeans, and she has to admit, it's not too bad.

She's still swinging her hips when she emerges from the lobby. It's super hot already. She might regret the jeans, even if she manages to stay on the shady side of the street, but wolf whistles from a couple of guys on a scaffold change her mind. She grins and waves, wondering what her outraged twenty-year-old self would say. Back then, and new to feminism, she'd likely have rounded up a few friends, made some anti-harassment placards, and staged a protest, right here on the street. Today, these guys just made up for a bad hair day.

She thought about taking John to Cafe Brauer today, to be more romantic. She often detours through the park and passes it on her way, and she'd be lying if she said it never crossed her mind as a great wedding venue. But meeting him at the Blarney Stone makes more sense. He's there all day anyway. Saves having to prop old Tom up behind the bar so he can go on a break. Tom's the owner. Came over to the States on Noah's Ark, according to himself. Came into a windfall, managed to buy himself a bar. Not the greatest idea for an alcoholic. According to John, all he did was get drunk and give free drinks to his buddies. After they'd staggered out the door,

Tom would get maudlin singing old Irish songs and keep drinking until he passed out.

When John got the job, the place was nearly done for. There's still singing, but now it's young bands, looking to get a break. It's the place to go in Chicago. He's done a great job. She caught herself last night watching him while The River were playing like it was their last day on earth. The crowd was going crazy, dancing when there wasn't really room, faces red with exuberance and drink, elbows colliding and beers splashing, and there was John, moving through them, around them, taking charge, taking care, totally handling it. When he caught her watching, he winked, and she was like the luckiest woman in the bar, in the city, on the planet. It was that kind of moment. Game-changing.

To her everlasting shame, when he first noticed her, she was literally crying into her beer, over Robin. It was really, truly over, she swore to Susie over her fourth – or was it fifth? – bottle of Corona. Susie was doing everything she could not to say *good riddance*, knowing as she did that it had been really, truly over several times before, only to start up again the next time *that dickhead* felt like playing away again.

Robin. The less said about that lost decade the

better. Brand new to teaching, she was grateful for his insider tips. Don't leave food in the staff room's fridge unless you want to share it with Mr Wallace. Get the report cards done right away so the parents are not on your case. Stay away from Mrs Dubois, the cranky vice-principal, on principle with a capital LE – his little joke, much reused, since he himself was the principal, and her boss. She only figured out he was married after they'd started *grabbing a bite* after work every Friday, and the *bite* had developed into sex back in her apartment. This was right before she was about to take him to meet her parents, too.

He wasn't happy in his marriage. He hadn't known it until he met her. He hated deceiving her. He hated deceiving his wife. Only, now she was having to deceive everyone too. Her mom and dad were total Catholics, for Chrissakes. They'd even started hinting about grandkids, but they sure wouldn't want them this way. The only one she could confide in was her old friend, Susie. But despite Susie's carefully phrased advice urging caution, she was naive enough to think Robin meant what he said, and it took her two full years before she grew leery of his lines. Then he promised he would leave his wife. Vicky hated herself when he talked about his wife, not to mention his kids, and she tells herself that they were already serious about each other by the time she found out.

She lost count of the number of times she ended it, and when she finally did, he fell apart; made a huge scene in the staff room, of all places, declared that she was the one he really loved, begged her to give him another chance. She went back after recess, reeling. This wasn't the life she had planned.

As soon as her class had gone home for the day, she handed in her notice and phoned Susie to meet her after work.

When she first noticed John, they had been in the bar for quite a few hours, and it had taken its toll. The big, good looking barman was leaning against the restroom door-jamb.

—I hope he was worth it, were his first words to her, or maybe they were to Susie, who was holding her hair.

Her response was to heave the foamy contents of her stomach into the toilet.

—She doesn't usually drink this much, she heard Susie say, before the next queasy wave overtook her.

—So it seems.

When she was well enough to leave the toilet cubicle John turned out the lights in the bar and insisted on driving them both home.

When she went back to the Blarney Stone two days later to thank him, he said she was grand, whatever that meant. When she asked if she could have a coffee, he asked her if she could handle it.

When she put the steaming cup to her lips, one of her better features, he said

—Of all the bars in all the world you had to walk into mine, and she finally laughed.

They drifted into dating. He wasn't sure he was staying in the US at that stage. He'd only had a J1 Visa, years before, and it had long expired. She made sure he understood that she was coming out of a long relationship and was therefore fragile, and probably not properly over Robin. Later, when she fessed up that Robin was married and she was damaged goods, flawed, morally compromised, he said he'd gathered that much from listening to her and Susie the first night.

A one-woman man, he told her with a grin when her experience with Robin prompted her to check early on if he was seeing other women. Just so she'd know where she stood. It hadn't taken long to figure out that John deployed his easy manner and ready wink freely. It was just his way. But if he flirted with his customers it was fine by her since it meant she didn't have to feel responsible for him. Let him flirt. She was already in her mid-thirties by then, and she didn't want to look like some desperate reproductive time-bomb waiting to detonate in the arms of an unsuspecting younger man, even if it was just by four years. Sometimes she let weeks go by without seeing him, a kind of deliberate game. Would he still be there when she came back? She almost willed him to see other women. But she did so knowing that behind his bar-banter and ready compliments he was totally solid.

She's often thought about finishing it. She wants things she's afraid to ask him for, things she's afraid even to want, in case she might get them. She's found herself thinking more and more about a house with a garden, nothing fancy, just enough space for a couple of kids to run around. But she's probably too old. And anyway, what's the point? It's all so fragile. Too much room for getting hurt. Besides, after all these years, she doesn't even know how he is around kids. His nephew and nieces are all in Ireland, but he never sees them because he's afraid he won't be able to get back into the States. When they started dating, Susie warned her that he might try to use her to get a green card, though after a while she had to admit that there didn't seem to be much danger of that.

Mostly she's just glad to be around him, and some days she can't imagine him not being there. Like when Kane went missing a couple of months back. One day he was there at his desk, next day he was missing. And the next, and the next. She knew right away something was up. He was the kind of kid who just didn't miss school. Finally the school board was investigating, calling her in. What did she know?

According to them, she knew enough that she should've reported it to the principal.

—Report what? she asked the board, feeling like a six-year-old herself.

Miss Kepple looked over the frames of her glasses and frowned. She was about Vicky's age, single, and as good an advertisement for getting married and having a family as any.

—Ms Delorente, as I'm sure you are aware, the safety of the children in our care is our first priority . . .

Like it wasn't hers. Like she was somehow involved in the disappearance of the little boy. She loves those kids. And Kane especially, he's a sweet kid. Multilingual, even if he doesn't . . . didn't say much. Quiet. Took her a month to get a smile out of him. His dad German, his mom Japanese. But they made sure to speak English around him, too. Too bad they couldn't manage to sort themselves out, in any language. Divorced midway through Kane's first grade. No wonder the kid was finding it hard to smile.

After the divorce, they both came to talk to her, separately. We want to do what's best for Kane. Dad's all worked up, starts crying because he wants to be part of his son's life and his wife – sorry, ex-wife – was making problems.

Seems when he got his girlfriend pregnant the Japanese wife kicked him out.

Maybe it was her own experience with Robin that stopped her from reporting how the mom was hanging around the school all the time, outside the gates, just out of sight of the schoolyard. Vicky could see her out of the corner of her eye when she stood facing the class. She didn't say anything, just felt sorry for her mostly. Dad had already gotten late picking Kane up when it was his week, so it was mostly Mom anyway. Guess Dad got real busy and she was just making sure Kane was safe.

She hates herself when she's like this. A bitter old maid like Miss Kepple. Sometimes she thinks the whole thing with Robin put her off men altogether, damaged her even, if that's not being too dramatic.

John's good for her, easy going. Doesn't hold stuff against her, or against anyone really. When the board was through grilling her, she went straight to see him. He got off work without asking any questions, and they drove to the lake.

The wind carried a chill from Canada, even though it was nearly June. She shivered.

—Are you all right, Vicky? John asked. Here. You're shaking.

He pulled his sweater off and wrapped it around her, and his simple concern was suddenly too much. She turned and buried her face in his T-shirt and sobbed with great heaving gasps. It was all so hopeless. She pictured serious little Kane, his lost-looking

mom, even his idiot dad. She even felt sorry for
Robin, and his blonde, elegant wife. It was all so
fucked up. What was the point of any of it? She cried
herself out, and when she finally lifted her head a
string of snot followed her, still attached to his shirt.

—Well, I haven't got a hanky, he said. Looks like
we're stuck with each other now.

She managed a laugh.

—Come on, he said, swiping it away with the
back of his hand and wiping it on his jeans. Let's
go some place you're not freezing.

They found a cafe a block up. Away from the lake
and back in the sun she struggled to articulate what
had got her so upset. What had triggered it? The
board meeting was part of it, for sure. Maybe because
it had come so soon after bumping into Joe Martello
at the Farmers' Market. That was unsettling, but she
thought she'd handled it OK. Even had a casual chat
with his girlfriend. Giving the *I'm not a threat* vibe
all round. She'd put it out of her mind until now, as
she'd always carefully kept Joe Martello out of her
mind.

—Take your time, John said, draping an arm along
the back of her chair. Tom can't do too much harm
to the bar in the middle of the afternoon.

—It's just they made me feel like I wasn't fit to . . .
Like all the bad things that happen to kids are my
fault. It just . . . brought up stuff. Kane's mom

abducted him, most like. It doesn't take a genius to figure it out. They're probably back in Japan by now. Can't blame her either.

He shrugged, neither agreeing nor disagreeing. Sometimes he drove her crazy, sitting on the fence, but mostly she liked that he saw the best in everyone. Even her. Especially her. A memory of Robin's kids shot through her, the one time she had seen them. The whole family together, getting into their car, two towheads, image of their mom. Robin, leaning across to buckle their seat belts, ruffling his son's hair. She ended the affair the next day for a second time, or was it a third?

—Maybe it's because of—

—You're a good teacher. The best. You're a natural with those kids. He hesitated. Maybe it's time to let the whole . . . Robin thing, go?

Six years on, he wasn't wrong. A few weeks with John was all it had taken to get over Robin. But instead of making her feel better, this had made her feel even worse. All her investment, all the risk, the pain, the heartbreak, those blond kids – even if they were nearly college age by now – for it not to even have been worth it? What did that say about her?

—That's easier said—

—Not really, Vick.

She looked up in surprise at his firm tone. Usually

he just let her talk, and he listened. It was what he was best at, that and pouring beer.

—What I'm saying is. You can feel bad about it forever, but it's just a small part of the picture. I mean, you're great with kids. I've seen them crowding around you at going-home time. That little kid, I bet he'll remember you as his favourite teacher, wherever he is now. They love you.

He took her hand.

—*I* love you. I mean . . . He looked embarrassed. What I'm saying is . . . What I'm asking is . . .

It was the longest serious speech she had heard him make.

—What, John?

He grinned.

—Well, how would you like to be buried with my people?

She looked at him blankly.

—I'm asking you to marry me, woman.

At first she was stuck for words. After all this time, she just hadn't seen it coming. As far as she was concerned, he was as ambivalent about committing as she was.

—Wow. What brought this on?

He picked up a sachet of sugar and began toying with its contents through the paper wrapping.

—Well, there was Robin . . .

—Bloody Robin, she thought, said.

108

He nodded.

—But then . . . I mean . . . I didn't want you to think . . . Well, the green card . . .

She had never seen him so unsure of himself. He was still fidgeting with the sachet, shaking the sugar back and forth like a demented maraca. So that was all it was about.

—So all this time . . . ?

—So, I'd have asked you in a heartbeat six months after I met you.

The sachet tore, and the white grains spilt across the table between them. Vicky absently wetted a finger and touched it to the sugar, then put the sweetness to her lips, as she tried to take this in.

—I didn't know . . .

—So . . . ?

—*Buried with your people.* I haven't heard that before.

She was buying time. She knew it and he knew it.

—Yea, it's gas, isn't it? He sounded miserable, and Vicky didn't know how to fix it.

—I need a little time . . .

It was the best she could do.

What was she, crazy? John's good looking, good in bed, good to her, just plain good, period. But did she want marriage, even to an all round good guy?

Kids. Did John want kids? What if he didn't? What if she didn't? Sure, she had this vague idea of a house, a family, but she hadn't really thought it through, hadn't thought she needed to. Realistically, she saw herself winding up in her apartment alone, with or without John somewhere in the background. Hell, they hadn't even gotten around to moving in together. Talked about it at one stage, when they'd been together a year, but they couldn't decide who should give up their apartment. She owned hers; he rented. He staged a bit of a macho stand, not wanting to be a kept man, she shrugged it off, and the subject was dropped. It's obvious now that she should've offered to get a place together.

You're not taking anything for granted, she tells her reflection in a store window as she sashays down North Clark. He might've changed his mind, lady.

But she's pretty sure he hasn't. Suddenly she wants to hear his voice. She's just twenty minutes from the Blarney Stone, but she takes out her cellphone.

—Hey, she says.

—Hello you.

—Just wanted to say hi. And . . . I miss you.

—You still in bed?

She can hear that he's turned away, probably from Tom, or some customer.

—Yeah. Totally naked. And I want you. Right now.

He groans.

—Ah, Jaysus, Vick, don't do that to a man.

—All right, all right. If you're not going to satisfy my womanly needs, how about you make me a coffee? I'm on my way over.

The El rattles past and half-drowns out what he says, but over the noise she makes out,

— . . . Jaysus sake, put some clothes on first.

She can't stop smiling as she hangs up.

She's about to put the phone back into her purse when she notices that she has a new message.

Áine

In the end it was desire that made her decision for her. Joe had left his mark all right. She booked her leave, six full weeks, under the disapproving stare of the woman in HR, who wanted to know what she planned to do with all that time off.

Mind your own business, you old bat.

—Just taking a break, she said. From the monotony and blouse ironing and form filling that you'll be doing while I'm getting well and truly laid, she added silently.

Conor had said he would take Daisy. Of course he would. He wanted to spend as much time with his daughter as he could. These formative years were so important, didn't Áine realise? Only now he's got his fluffy-haired girlfriend pregnant, and Lucy thinks they should spend as much time together as they can before the baby arrives, and mightn't Daisy feel a bit in the way?

Áine drizzles extra-virgin olive oil over her baby leaf and cherry tomato salad, and puts a forkful to her lips. It tastes of nothing. *Another time, Áine*, were Conor's parting words as he drove out of her driveway in his stupid little Yaris. There might never be another time. She's toed the line for thirty-five years. Her ticket is bought. The time is now. She stabs at a tomato and it shoots out of the bowl, leaving a patchy, oily trail across the counter.

She's thought about asking Maeve, but they go down to Wexford every summer with Robbie's family, and the other kids are all older than Daisy. Nana, Áine's mum, has Lanzarote booked for a fortnight and half a dozen mini-breaks besides. She's stuck, her empty six weeks stretching out ahead of her like a sentence. She pushes her uneaten lunch away. Checking that Daisy's still glued to *Dora the Explorer*, she goes up to the spare room to break the news to Joe.

She hopes he can't see her self-pitying tears welling up, but she needn't worry, he's not even looking at her. He's watching TV somewhere out past his computer screen. In place of *Hi* she gets

—Go Lance.

When she tells him what's happened, though, he breaks away sharply from the cycling.

—Bring her, he says, through the mouthful of sunflower seeds he's steadily feeding himself.

—Bring her?

—Sure. Why not. Farms are for families. Kids running around . . . House is plenty big . . . Go Lance!

She pauses, imagining Daisy skipping along the strawberry rows, getting lots of fresh air and sunshine, learning how things grow. But the house. It's plenty big all right, but it's a tip.

—But it's not exactly fit for a child. Or an adult . . .

He does not look amused.

—Joking, she adds.

—It'll be straightened out by July, he says coldly, and turns again to his cycling.

It's not really enough, but now he's all offended, it'll have to do.

She emails later, apologising for being negative about the house, telling him that she has to think of Daisy. She doesn't mean the apology – she's being diplomatic – but Joe's in better form this time. Lance must've won his race. He admits that the house is less than perfect, and promises he will get it straightened out by July.

The night before they're flying out she remembers something else. She phones Joe. She can hear voices in the background. Must be the students he told her were starting work today.

—The, em, smoking . . . ?

—Yes, Áine? He sounds impatient. He doesn't like being interrupted, and in fairness he can't exactly talk about it in front of his employees.

—Em, not in front of Daisy, the smoking? Is that all right?

—Yes, fine. Gotta go.

He's less than perfect, whispers a voice in her head which sounds a bit like Maeve's, a bit like her own before she decided to look for adventure. He's abrupt, rude if she gets him in the wrong mood; then the next minute he's sorry, he's lonely, and he's begging her to come out, reminding her how good they are together. Talking, talking, talking. More than once over the past couple of months, she'd toyed with the idea of placing the phone down on the counter and coming back five minutes later to see if he'd notice.

It shocks her that she's thinking like this when they're about to get on a plane in the morning to spend six weeks with him in Illinois. She tries to push her reservations down, like a jack into its box, but they keep slipping from under her hand and popping back out. This is partly to do with Daisy. You have to introduce new ideas to kids delicately. Too much too soon and they make themselves sick with excitement; not enough preparation and they freak out on you. So, once she decided to bring her, she filtered the plan slowly, letting Daisy come to terms with it one step at a time.

But now her new *Dora the Explorer* backpack is stuffed with her favourite toys and books. She has a new passport, and a premium-price ticket. They're going.

Not just because of Daisy. And not because of Joe, either. They're going because Áine has sat at the same desk in the same office talking to the same people about the same nothing for long enough, and now she just wants something to happen.

Her second thoughts begin when they arrive at O'Hare and Daisy sets eyes on Joe for the first time. They approach each other warily, sizing each other up. Before the words come out of Daisy's mouth, Áine knows they're coming, and she can't stop them.

—He's dirty, Mummy. Daisy's clear child's voice rings out around Arrivals.

—Shh, Daisy, don't be rude, Áine says under her breath, smiling at Joe as he gets closer.

His shorts look like the same ones he was wearing back in May, and they look like he hasn't taken them off since. The T-shirt is frayed at the neck and so old that she can't make out what was written on it.

—But why is he so dirty?

Joe raises his eyebrows at Áine as if to ask what she is going to do about her rude kid. It hadn't occurred to her to wonder what he's like around children. Or even to ask what his childhood was like. He'd told her he was an only child, but that was about it. She hopes she's not making a terrible mistake.

—Joe works on a farm, Daisy. Farm work is dirty. And it's clean dirt . . .

Please don't ask why he didn't get changed to come pick us up.

When they get to the car, she thinks, Please don't ask why it's such a mess. She's annoyed with Joe. There isn't even room on the back seat for Daisy. He moves piles of flattened boxes and rubbish for her to sit down.

—Went by the wholesalers on my way, he says. Not to waste a trip.

Waste?

She's relieved when Daisy falls asleep in the car straight away.

Daisy has woken up full of energy when they reach the farm, her body clock all over the place, so when Joe says he wants to show her around outside, Áine agrees. It's nice to see her so curious, and Joe lapping up her questions. *What is this for? Where are the* cows? *What are all those people doing?* He's patient, explaining to her the way he would to an adult. Áine starts to relax, forcing herself to push away the bad feeling she still has about the house. They're on holiday, after all. *This is all going into vetch after the season. Soil needs crop rotation, otherwise it gets all tired and used up. Vetch's as good a cover-crop . . .* Áine lets his voice wash over her. It's nice here, like he said it would be. The evening is warm and everything is pastel-coloured in the setting sun. There are people milling around, laughing and joking with each other, getting into their cars, driving off. She spots Rick, the mature student, and waves, enjoying his surprise at seeing her again. He waves back, and looks like he's coming over, but then, with a look to Joe, he changes his mind and turns away again.

They're students and wwoofers, and they're going home after a day of picking tomatoes and strawberries, Joe is explaining to Daisy. He shows her the full trays stacked in the cooler, ready for tomorrow's market. It doesn't occur to him that she might like to eat one, but that's only because he isn't used to kids, Áine reasons.

In the barn, Carlos is twisting papery husks off tomatillos, then putting them into trays. He is unable to hide his surprise at seeing her again. Or maybe it's because she's brought Daisy. When Joe follows them in, Carlos looks back down at what he is doing.

—Getting those tomatillos ready, Carlos? Joe says unnecessarily.

—*Sí*.

—Yea, Joe says, at a loss for a moment. Mm hm.

The barn creaks and expands in the warmth of the evening.

—Can I do that? Daisy asks Carlos.

—Let Carlos do his work, Joe says. We have to go see the hoophouses.

Carlos says something in Spanish. Joe looks flustered. *Sí, sí,* he's saying, but Áine can see he's struggling.

—In English? Carlos asks.

—Been trying to learn Spanish, Joe tells Áine, looking embarrassed. *Sí*, in English, he says to Carlos.

—Rick want to talk to you before he goes home.

Joe looks like he doesn't know whether to stay or go. In the end, he leaves, telling them to wait here.

Carlos hands Daisy a tomatillo. She studies it carefully. Then she looks at him for guidance.

—Like this, *sí*?

Daisy nods. She turns one of the boxes over and sits down, then she grips the tomatillo and twists. The wrinkled brown cover comes off. She holds it up to Carlos, and he nods his approval.

—Is sticky, no?

Daisy opens and closes her hand a few times, feeling the tackiness, and nods. She puts the tomatillo carefully into the tray and reaches for another. Carlos laughs.

—She is a good worker.

Áine remembers that Carlos has daughters too. She asks him about them.

—They are older than this little one. Much older. But still they are my little girls. Still need to take care, he adds, looking at Daisy.

Joe's back, looking agitated.

—Damn Swedes, want to stay in town at Rick's. They all want to stay with Rick. What's wrong with staying in the farmhouse? Does it not make sense to stay in the farmhouse when you're working on the farm? Áine?

Carlos has become as engrossed in his task as Daisy. It's up to Áine to make agreeable noises, but she has a good idea why the Swedes want to stay with Rick. Besides, it suits her. She doesn't particularly relish the idea of sharing the house, and Joe, with a bunch of strangers.

The smell hits them as soon as they step onto the porch. That damn downstairs toilet. She was foolish enough to go in there the last time she was here. It was like something out of *Trainspotting*. All the workers used it and nobody cleaned it, Joe had explained without a trace of irony.

—Eeeww. Daisy wrinkles her nose.

Thankfully Joe's gone on ahead to put their bags upstairs. A glance towards the kitchen confirms what Áine feared. Exactly as she left it in May. She's glad they didn't eat the flapjacks and snacks she'd packed for the plane, because it might be their dinner. She holds Daisy's hand tighter and leads her upstairs.

They find Joe in the doorway of the big front room, the master bedroom, probably, if it was a normal house. His own bedroom is over the kitchen, at the back. He has his arms full with boxes of preserves.

—Just give me five, he says with a sheepish grin as he passes them. You'll have some space in no time.

—Jesus. She takes in the room where her daughter is supposed to sleep. There's no floor space to be seen, just towers of boxes stacked everywhere. Perched on one of the highest piles she sees a rolled sleeping bag and a camping mat. Straightened out by July, my arse. Daisy looks like she might cry.

—Don't worry, sweetie. We'll get it sorted. It'll be an adventure. You'll be just like Dora.

—Dora's adventures are not like this, Daisy says.

Áine sits her on the window sill and unzips her Dora bag. She takes out the bedraggled bear Daisy takes everywhere.

—Here, Daisy, here's Mr Snuggly. Have a look at one of your books for a few minutes and I'll get everything all organised. You'll be as snug as a bug in no time.

She goes out to search for Joe.

—Five minutes, he says, holding up five fingers to preempt her approach, and her reprimand. Sooner if you help. I did clean the bathroom, Áine. Time just got away from me . . . He flashes his grin.

It doesn't take long to move the boxes after all, and she's mollified when she sees that he has actually done a half-decent job on the bathroom. Maybe he'll keep up the good work downstairs, she suggests. He looks, to check whether she's serious. Before he turns to leave, he nods towards their passports where Áine's left them on the window sill.

—It's probably better not to leave them lying around with so many people coming and going from the farm. Want me to stick those in the safe?

—Em, OK, Áine agrees.

Daisy's already starting to fade when Áine stands her into the bath for a quick wash, and then she's happy enough to climb into the sleeping bag with Mr Snuggly. She's just dozing off, and Áine's starting to tiptoe out to go look for Joe, when Daisy shoots up, her eyes the size of moons.

—Mummy, Mummy, why are the birds still chirruping in the night?

She listens. There is definite chirping and, more ominously, scratching, coming from overhead.

—Joe? she calls in a loud whisper.

—'S up? He appears in the doorway, joint in hand, which instantly annoys her. Daisy wasn't to see any evidence of his smoking. He agreed. But she called him in, after all. She lets it go.

—What's . . . ? She turns her eyes upwards.

Daisy is looking anxiously from one to the other. She is prone to nightmares anyway. Áine is forever trying to convince her that there is nothing in the dark that isn't there in the daytime. She knows how her daughter's little heart is racing now.

He laughs.

—That's the bats. They can't get in the house.

—Bats, Daisy breathes. She does not look reassured.

—Can you not get rid of them?

He looks surprised at the idea, then shrugs,

—Sure.

He turns and leaves. To shoo out the bats, Áine presumes, but when she hears nothing she tells Daisy she'll be right back. She follows him into his den where he's watching TV and smoking.

—The *bats,* Joe? she whispers.

—Whaddya want me to do? It's late. I'll get rid of them, OK? I'll call pest control tomorrow.

—Fine, she says sulkily, realising he's right, there is nothing he can do tonight. But I'm sleeping in with Daisy. She's terrified.

—Mm hm, he says, and turns back to his basket-ball game.

The next morning Daisy is sitting out on the porch, engrossed in her first encounter with a Pop-Tart, and Joe has already gone out to the farm, so Áine ascends the steep, narrow steps to the attic to see for herself. The door at the top of the stairs seems to be locked. The more the knob resists, the more vividly she imagines what might be on the other side. Nothing that's not there in the day, she tells herself sternly, shooing the images away. The door hinges, stiff with lack of use, finally yield, and the door creaks open.

There are no decomposing women. But the stench, and the inches-deep bat shit the door had to push against to open, make her stomach contract as much as if there had been. She suppresses the urge to gag. There's a bit of a rustle, but otherwise nothing is wrong with the room but dirt. It's spacious, and would even be bright if the crust of cobwebs and dust was cleaned off the roof windows. It would make a lovely bedroom, up under the eaves. You could lie in bed looking at the stars. If it wasn't for the bats. And the dirt. The place is filthy. Fine, it's just the attic, but he didn't keep his promise to get the house ready. It's not good enough.

She storms down the attic stairs and out to the

sheds, where Joe is explaining hydroponics to a group
of workers.

—Can I have a word?

Joe lets his auctioneer's spiel die.

—Daisy can't stay in a house like that.

He looks her up and down slowly, from her rigid
face to her folded arms and firmly planted feet. She
can feel the colour rising to her face, and perspiration
begins to dampen her armpits. The workers are
watching everything. She decides to push it.

—It's the house, and the bats. They'll have to go
or . . . Anyway, I think I'd like to keep our passports
with our stuff.

As soon as she says it, she knows it's a mistake.
She just can't tell how much of one.

Joe glares at her, then turns back to the waiting men.

—You got to control solution levels . . .

She unclenches and unfolds and skulks away back
up to the house. Even in her anger, she notices that
he knows an awful lot about hydroponics. She takes
deep breaths. She'll take Daisy for a walk, get away
from the smell of the downstairs loo.

When they get back, they pass Rick leaving the
downstairs toilet, carrying a bucket of cleaning things
and a mop. He doesn't look happy. The place does
smell better though. How hard was that?

She decides not to bring up the subject of the bats
when Joe comes in for lunch.

—How'd ya like mac 'n' cheese? he asks Daisy.

—I don't know, she says. She's sitting up on the table, something she's not allowed to do at home.

—You don't know mac 'n' cheese? What kind of kid doesn't know mac 'n' cheese. Here you go—

He throws down a box from the cupboard. Áine holds her breath, but Daisy catches it easily. Áine hadn't known her reflexes were that good. She supposes she has Conor to thank, since he's the one who plays catch with her. Or used to, now his girlfriend's having a baby. She's arrested by a half-formed and completely unexpected image of Joe throwing ball with Daisy out in the field, after all the workers have gone home, against the peachy pink evening sky.

—Hey Daze, he says, bursting Áine's peachy bubble. The pet name rankles. He doesn't know Daisy well enough for that.

—What about we check out those bats? Show your mom you're not scared.

He holds out a hand to her. Daisy freezes. She looks to Áine.

—I don't think she's ready yet, she tries.

—Come, he tells Daisy, ignoring Áine. There's nothing to be afraid of.

Daisy doesn't move.

—She doesn't want to go.

—It'll be good for her.

He takes hold of Daisy's hand and slides her off the table. She begins to whimper.

—She's *afraid*. Let her go.

—Who's afraid? he asks softly. He lets go of Daisy and gets down on his hunkers to talk to her at her level.

—You don't have to go, Daze. But just think how brave you'd feel if you had a peep up there, saw for yourself there's nothing to worry about. You'd be just like that girl on your backpack, what's her name again?

—Dora, Daisy says in a small voice.

—That's right, Dora. You'd be cool like Dora. Hey, doesn't Dora wear . . .

He takes off his baseball cap and puts it onto Daisy's head. It comes right down over her eyes. She giggles and pushes it off.

—Dora doesn't have a hat.

He feigns surprise.

—Dora doesn't have a hat? I'll have it back in that case. Say, why don't we do the bat thing some other time? I'm a little tired right now. He gives a big, fake yawn and Daisy giggles again.

He stands up and, with a cold look to Áine, goes to the fridge, takes out two beers, and goes upstairs.

Daisy falls asleep in the heat of the afternoon after devouring her mac 'n' cheese. Áine takes a beer out of the fridge herself and goes outside to sit in the shade of the porch. It's nice there, sipping the cold, tasteless beer and watching the world – well, the students – go by. And there's Carlos, on his way into the processing shed. The two blond lads shovelling manure into a barrow must be the Swedes. The smell reaches her all the way here. It must be payback from Joe for moving in with Rick. Áine smiles. After a while, she reasons she has nothing to gain by staying mad at Joe. She goes up to find him. He's in the den, where else?

—Hey, she says.

—Hey.

To break the awkwardness, Áine picks up a black-and-white photo from the table where it's lying face down, covered in dust. It's a little boy in a dicky bow, seated at a piano. He's looking down, as if he's shy around whoever's holding the camera. The woman beside him – his teacher? – is half turned, her dark eyes unfathomable.

—You?

He takes it carefully out of her hands and puts it down on the floor beside his recliner, face down. His expression is the same as the woman's. His mother?

—Ah-ah, Áine, he says, wagging a finger at her.

The photo is out of bounds, then. She shrugs that she doesn't care. She doesn't. Only why does everything with Joe have to be a big mystery?

There's a momentary stand-off before he grins and reaches for her waist.

—Come here.

He pulls her onto his lap, then they're kissing and shedding their clothes and climbing all over each other in a frenzy of saliva and sweat and sex.

Joe's farm is surrounded by the cornfields he despises so much. He takes her out in them the second afternoon of their stay. Not that he wants to. He's furtive about where he's going, muttering something about taking a stroll. He'd told her on Skype how he liked to hike for days in the Rockies, described the clean, thin air and endless space, his lungs labouring and legs protesting but going on and on. He was practically spouting poetry, talking about camping under glittering black skies, until she was longing to try it for herself, and she managed to extract a half-promise from him that they'd go hiking at the end of the summer. But *taking a stroll* wasn't very Joe. She checks on Daisy, a sweaty bundle in her sleeping bag, fast asleep, then wanders downstairs and outside to have a look for him. She spots him heading out into the cornfields.

—OK if I tag along?

He doesn't look pleased.

—Fine.

She has to trot behind him, noting that he doesn't

129

bother to hold leaves out of the way for her. Equality, and all that. They're not ripe yet, but they're a couple of feet taller than her, and they create a lovely, greenish light where they're walking. Joe is pressing on like a man on a mission, and she's soon hot and dusty and wondering why she's bothered. She wonders if Daisy's still sleeping. She thinks she might head back, and calls his name.

The plants ahead stop rustling. She can feel him waiting for her. Maybe they'll make love, if that's what you'd call their frantic couplings. Out here in the corn, that'd be exciting. Maybe she can stay a little longer after all. But when she catches up, he turns on her, his face dark with anger.

—Shut the fuck up, he says in a furious whisper.

She stops, shocked, as if he slapped her. She's between tears and turning around, back to the house and straight to the airport, which she can see him register.

—I'm sorry, he says, shaking his head sadly. I shouldn't have spoken to you like that. Sometimes I let the pressure get to me.

She sniffs.

—Here.

He's holding out a wad of paper towels, the ones he helps himself liberally to every time he gets petrol, *gas*. She takes one delicately from the pile and blows her nose.

—Better?

She nods, though it's not true, she's not better. She's still annoyed.

—What pressure? She has to try hard to keep her tone neutral. She's not completely successful, because his eyes flash briefly, but then he seems to make a decision. He takes her hands in his.

—Come, Áine. I want to show you something. But we need to keep quiet.

She glances back towards the house, wondering if Daisy's all right. Another few minutes should be OK.

This time he is solicitous of her, moving leaves aside, checking that she is all right. Now and then he pauses. He seems to be listening for something. Just as she's beginning to think they will never find their way out, they arrive at the edge of the field. There's a stream, with wild purple flowers – foxgloves, she thinks – growing among the bushes and peeping out of the long grasses.

—It's beautiful, she says, careful this time to speak quietly.

Joe takes no notice. He's guiding her down to the sides of the stream – under the bushes, where it's mucky and her new sandals will be destroyed – but she thinks better of asking why they can't just stay on the higher ground. She doesn't want to risk annoying him again.

131

At last he stops, listens, then leaves the cover of the bushes. She stumbles up the bank after him, and when she joins him he appears to have arrived at his intended destination. She doesn't know what's special about here. It's just more long grass, more bushes.

—It's a weed, he's saying in a low voice. Vivacious. Will grow in spite of you, long as it gets eight hours sunlight a day.

He's talking fast. The bush he's referring to is pretty, its feathery, serrated leaves spreading out in stars. He's peering into it, turning leaves over, plucking some here and there.

—Practically take care of themselves. Natural habitat. Need plenty of water at this stage though.

Now he's looking about in the undergrowth, then finds what he's looking for: a bucket, hidden out of sight. He sprints to the stream and fills it up, talking the whole time.

—Around the roots. See? Like this. About half a bucket. He looks about him until he sees the next bush like it, then he empties the bucket around its base and turns back to the stream to refill.

—Ideal conditions. Water. Cover – the corn camouflages the plants. Don't want to alert Mike. His cornfields.

Áine's brain at last catches up with his spiel. It occurs to her that this is a kind of lesson, and that she's supposed to be paying attention.

—Are they marijuana plants?

As soon as she's asked she knows it was a stupid question. She can see him do a split-second evaluation, as if he's wondering if she's for real.

—Yes, Áine, they are. They are marijuana plants.

He waits for her to react. She is determined not to look shocked, though she is shocked. She didn't mind that he smoked the stuff non-stop, but growing it was different. She wonders if the joint she smoked came from here. If that made her an accomplice . . .

—How many . . . ? she asks finally.

He grins.

—Is it for my own personal use, you mean? Medicinal, preferably? No, Áine, it is not for my own personal use. I sell it – most of it, at least.

Whereas before all she saw was pretty flowers and cornfields and the stream, now that she knows what to look for her eyes are able to pick out the plants everywhere. Her thoughts go straight to Daisy.

—So, you're a drug dealer?

Joe switches out of his supercilious tone and speaks, still fast, but more gently, persuasively.

—You can see how hard I work just to keep the place going. And just wait until you see when the season really gets underway. It's non-stop then. Four a.m. starts for the markets, then managing all these workers. Keeping on top of supplies, trips to the wholesalers. It's flat out.

He's talking flat out now too.

—The mortgage, it's a big whack. The strawberries, the asparagus, the tomatoes, the basil, they just about cover wages. You can see that. You're not stupid.

—But you've been at it for years, she can't help interjecting, if only to shut him up. She needs to think. And it's clearly not a viable business, her civil servant's voice adds silently.

He has the grace to look slightly ashamed.

—It's not so simple, Áine. It's about spreading the wealth, doing something worthwhile, something for the planet. You know how I feel about the farm. It's my child. It's my Daisy. It's what keeps me going. It provides good food for people who care about good food. It provides work, well-paid work, for Carlos and all the others.

—But you can't keep going if it's never going to pay its way. The banks . . . Don't you get audited or something?

—I make payments to my dad, not the banks, he mutters, not looking at her now. I make the payments to my dad. He got a shit-load of cash when he sold shares in the dealership. It'll all be mine eventually anyway. Better make use of it now, not leave it sitting earning interest for those fucks.

Áine is not sure which *fucks* he means.

—I know you're thinking, pathetic, forty years old and running to Daddy for handouts. And you're right, Áine. You're right to think that. I'm not proud of that. But I'm damned if he's going to know the farm's struggling. That's why I grow the plants. It's not for me. I don't make anything out of them for myself. Come fall, these plants are what pay for another year's rent. You think I want to be doing this? You think I like sneaking around my neighbour's corn? I'm just doing what I have to do.

He looks up at her at last, almost shy. Like the little boy in the photo. I was hoping . . . I mean . . . Will you stay? Will you think about it, at least? You can pretend you never saw the plants. It's why I didn't want you coming out here with me this evening. Daisy will never know. This . . . He waves his arm around. This won't be forever. The loan will be paid, and I stand to inherit . . . let's say quite a bit, when my dad dies.

—Is your dad very old?

—I guess he's in his seventies.

—That's not so old.

It's a strange conversation to be having. Like he wants his dad to die. Like she should want his dad to die, and that this would make everything OK. Wait, it's a strange conversation because they're talking about a marijuana crop.

He shrugs.

—Think about it, huh?

She gives him a wary smile, and says she will.

—So, uh . . . He scratches his beard. So . . . I guess I gotta get these guys watered. Think you can make it back by yourself?

She wants to get away. She needs to get back to Daisy anyway. She's been gone far longer than she meant to be. She nods.

—Good girl. He kisses her. Then he kisses her again, longer this time.

When she steps down onto the stream bank he is already examining the heart of one of his plants.

She retraces their steps as best she can, her head spinning. There's the fallen tree where they crossed the stream. She clambers up the bank to the edge of the cornfield. It's easy enough, once you're going in the right direction. You just follow the straight row. Even if you're going the wrong way, you'll come to a road or a boundary eventually. This is what she is telling herself sternly, but her heart is pounding. She feels as if she's swimming in a leafy sea, far out of her depth, with no shore in sight. Just keep going, just follow the row. Just breathe. But she can feel the panic rising from somewhere inside her, the part that is cut off from reason. The sweat that breaks out on her skin isn't coming from the heat of the sun, still high in the sky, but from deep within her, and it smells of fear.

She recognises the smell because she's been lost in the corn before: only, until now, she had forgotten.

She can't have been more than three years old. Her father was standing with a neighbour, both of them with their arms folded as they looked out across the field. Sounds occasionally rumbled out of the corners of their mouths. He didn't notice her wander off. The walls of corn were green, as high as houses, and went on forever, and no matter which way she turned, she was still lost, the big leaf-fingers folding down to touch her, whispering their secrets to her.

As she follows the row leading, she hopes, back to Joe's farm she can still hear her three-year-old self crying, can still smell her three-year-old's terror.

She hasn't decided what to do once she gets there. Straight back to the airport, never set foot in the place again? It's what Maeve would do.

And yet.

She can see the corn thinning and opening out, and as she emerges at the back of the hoophouses, careful to check that no one is around to see her, she can feel the *and yet* rising up in her like one of Joe's seedlings under a heat lamp. Because try as she might to think like Maeve, she can't deny the thrill she's feeling at the idea of living dangerously. Even if it's only vicarious, she qualifies. After all, the plants have nothing to do with her. It'd be a huge hassle to try and change the tickets at this stage, not to mention expense. It's just for a few weeks, a summer. And there's the hike he's half-promised, that she promised Daisy, and she never breaks her promises to Daisy. It'd be a shame to miss that. They've already picked out their new hiking shoes, splay-toed Keens for both of them, on the REI website. Joe isn't the worst. His intentions are good. He pays all his workers more than the average farm-labour rate. Carlos's family back in Mexico probably have a more comfortable life thanks to him. And he's certainly interesting.

She can still feel his mouth pressing hers. In spite of everything, she'll stay.

Above her head the stalks loom like giants, their thick leaves reaching down, trying to touch her with their tips. She pushes them aside, running first this way, then that, but their sharp edges are cutting and scratching at her face, her hands, her bare legs. She's panting and crying, smearing the sweat and dust around her eyes with her fists, calling *Daddy, Daddy, where are you?* Her face stings. She looks at her fist and sees blood there from the scratches. Now, the corn is coming alive. It wants to catch her. It's going to hurt her. She collapses onto the dirt, buries her head in her arms and sobs. Above her the corn leaves are folding down to touch her, whispering, whispering, whispering.

She wakes up still sobbing, drenched in sweat. She's been having the dream every night since Joe took her out in the corn. The first thing she does is to reach out for Daisy – there she is, right where she should be, sleeping peacefully, her cheeks reddened in the rapidly warming Illinois morning. Light is bursting through the gaps of the ill-fitting shutters. The sound of a tractor reaches the room where they are sleeping, unfamiliar insects creak and chirp, her daughter stretches and yawns. It takes Áine a few minutes to relegate the dream to where it belongs.

They go outside after breakfast. Daisy is barefoot, and wearing only a light, sleeveless daisy-print dress: her favourite. Áine has her slathered in sun cream, but in just three weeks she has steadily grown golden. Her hair has become streaked with the sun, too. She gets it from Conor; red-headed Áine only freckles and burns. It's great that Daisy can be out all day, roaming around free. If she was at home, she'd be stuck in the crèche all day. She pulls out her phone to take a photo to send to Maeve and her mother, evidence of the nice time they're having.

—There. You look very pretty. Come on, let's get some chores out of the way. It'll be fun.

—But I want to go with Carlos, Daisy complains, pulling away from the grip Áine has on her hand. Carlos has emerged from the barn, carrying a pile of plastic trays.

—Carlos is busy, sweetie. He has lots of work to do. She looks at him for confirmation.

—Is OK, he says, shrugging. He begins to walk down towards the hoophouses.

—Pleeeese, Mum. She breaks free and, without waiting for Áine's answer, races down the track after him.

He pretends to ignore her as she trails along behind him. But when they go inside the hoophouse – today he's picking chilli peppers – she sees him explaining carefully to Daisy that she shouldn't eat them, that they will burn her mouth. Then he rubs his eyes and points to the chillis. Daisy puts her hands behind her back and watches him, as good as gold. She's safe with Carlos.

Áine turns back to the farmhouse. The bats are still there, in spite of her pleas to Joe to get rid of them. Just thinking about them makes her shudder. He still hasn't called pest control, and she can't bring it up again. Daisy stopped talking about them too, probably because she's afraid Joe will want to bring her to see them, so it looks like they're there to stay.

She climbs the steps to the porch. Despite the bats,

despite the cornfields and their secret, she's still here, and she has laundry to hang out.

She unloads the washing machine into a basket and takes it out the back. Clothes are almost dry before you empty the basket here. Daisy's shorts and T-shirts are soon pegged onto the line, so she figures she might as well do another load. She goes back into the house and heads upstairs to round up towels and sheets, and maybe some of Joe's clothes – though he always seems to wear the same thing. She strips the big bed, not that anyone actually sleeps in it. They've had a few more hot encounters there, but he still sleeps in the den after, and she stays in the other room with Daisy. She made him take out all the boxes after the first night, then she scrubbed every inch of it until even the window panes sparkled.

She's been doing a lot of that lately. She can't bear a dirty house, and she has lots of time on her hands, so bit by bit she's been putting some order on Joe's farmhouse. She wonders if there's a domestic version of a wwoofer. She searches down behind the bed for stray socks. She can put up with it for another few weeks, then there's the promise of the Rocky Mountains. She's more or less pinned him down. She's been reading about the trail Joe told her about, in Big Horn, Wyoming, where you can hike to 13,000 feet. A thirteener, he called it. They'd have to drive a thousand miles, across four States, to get there, and she can't believe how much of a thrill it gives her. She was always a package-holiday kind of girl before, but now she's a pioneer, a character out of *Grapes of Wrath*, a Thelma. Or a Louise. Every day, she takes Daisy on a long walk to break in their Keens, and to see how far she can manage, and tells her about how much fun it is to go camping. Daisy's getting excited about it too.

The floor beneath the bed is covered in dust. She sneezes several times in succession. In for a penny, she thinks, and takes a dirty towel to give it a wipe. Her cleaning uncovers a cable, and she follows it with her towel, past the bed, to where it's been taped to the floor so you'd hardly notice it. She drops the towel into her basket, about to leave, when her eye catches the cable where it reappears, just for an inch or so, only to disappear again into a neatly drilled hole in the corner of the closet door.

She pauses half way to the laundry basket. There's something not right about that cable. She tells herself not to be ridiculous. But a cable in a closet? It doesn't make any sense. She goes over to the window and peers out around the farm yard. There's no sign of anyone. Then she goes out to the landing and listens; there's only the occasional creak of a door or a bat or whatever makes the sounds in Joe's old house.

She goes back to the closet and opens the door carefully. There's a pile of stuff on the floor, fallen clothes, a few books, the usual abandoned sports stuff, some dusty boxes. She slides the lid off one. Photos. The same little boy in the photo in the den. And the woman, his mother. He wasn't happy about her looking before, for whatever reason. She closes the box guiltily, keeping one ear out for any sound on the stairs. She picks up one of the books, *Growing Your Own Marijuana*, and flicks through it, and she's disconcerted to discover that she can actually recognise one or two of the varieties. As she puts it back she half-registers the college yearbook beneath it.

At first, she can't find where the cable enters the closet, but by feeling around under the mess, right in the back corner, her hand comes in contact with a flat, cool surface. She pushes off the clothes. It's a laptop. Not Joe's. At least, not the one he uses every day. It's in the den. Isn't it? She feels as if she has strayed into dangerous territory. Heart pounding, she jumps up and runs to check. There it is, recharging on top of the TV. It's nothing, there is nothing wrong, she tells herself.

She returns to the laptop in the closet. As she opens it with shaking hands, the crack of light that emanates from it seems to fill the closet like a beacon. But Joe won't be back for ages, she reassures herself. He hardly ever comes in before lunch, only if he needs to get money out of the safe to go pick up something from the store. It's open on his homepage. She goes to *History*. He isn't great with computers; his history is one long list of the same: http. *l'il cuties l'il cuties l'il cuties.*

A rush of dread runs through her and she runs to the toilet, where her bowels give away her fear. She flushes, then panics in case she missed hearing Joe come in in the noise of the rushing water. What if today was one of the rare days he did come back in?

She has an idea.

She runs downstairs, calling, not too loudly, as if she's just heard him come in.

—Joe? Joe?

There's no response, as she expects.

Next, she phones his cellphone.

—Joe?

—What's up, Áine? he asks in a whisper. He sounds annoyed.

As she thought – he's out with his plants.

—Oh, nothing. Just making a pot of coffee, wondered if you wanted a cup. Sorry. You're . . . ? She needs to know for sure.

—Yes, I'm.

—So . . . Should I save you some? Will you be long?

—No coffee. I haven't got there yet. I can't talk right now.

He hangs up.

He hasn't got to the plants yet. So she has at least half an hour. She rushes back up the stairs two at a time. She doesn't dare click on the site. Instead, she closes the laptop, puts it back into its dark corner and replaces the junk around it. She closes the closet door. She picks up her basket. Then she puts it back down and, feeling like a criminal, takes out the bedsheets and replaces them on the bed. She does the same with the dirty socks, dropping them down at the back of the mattress onto the floor. She doesn't want Joe to know she's been tidying in here. She wishes she could put the dust back.

She's in a swelter by the time she has covered her tracks. All she wants is a cool drink and somewhere she can go to think. Shit. The coffee. She races down to the kitchen. She scrapes the used grounds out of the pot and puts in fresh. Then she fills the pot base, screws on the top, and puts the pot on top of the stove, where it soon begins to gurgle and hiss. The smell makes her feel sick. She needs to think. It's possible that she's jumping to conclusions, like she did with the attic. After all, *l'il cuties* could be a website for kittens. Even if it was full-on, live, flesh-in-your-face porn, it wouldn't bother her. But the gnawing, sick feeling remains.

The coffee brewed, she pours a drop into a mug and leaves it on the table, then puts the rest down the sink. She has to know what *l'il cuties* is. It dawns on her that she can look it up on her own phone. She can hear voices coming from outside, which means it must be close to lunch for the workers, and Joe likes to be around to chat to them about what needs doing. He'll be back any minute.

She goes upstairs again and locks herself into the bathroom. Her fingers are shaking so much she's barely able to type in her search. *l i l c . . . l'il cuties,* Google suggests. She taps. Pictures of little girls. That's all. Sweet, Shirley Templesque little girls, in frilly dresses, smiling for the camera. She scrolls down. More pictures, lots and lots, and all more or less the same. Nothing sinister at all. What a relief. She closes the site and deletes her own history, just in case. But her heart is speeding out of control and her breaths are coming in short gasps.

She needs to find Daisy.

She rushes downstairs again, hoping she won't run into Joe. She races along the grassy path towards the hoophouse where she'd last seen her. It's steamy hot inside and the sweat is running off her as she searches up and down the rows. No one's there.

In the next hoophouse a couple of workers are desultorily picking tomatoes.

—Have you seen Daisy? she asks, trying to keep her voice steady. They shake their heads. She goes on to the next, but still no Daisy. She tells herself again, it's nothing, it's nothing. She clutches her phone as she runs frantically from one hoophouse to the next.

Think. Stop and think. Lunch. Of course. Daisy loves watching Carlos while he eats his lunch. She stares at whatever he has brought that day until he hands her a piece. Áine feels guilty about it, but he says it's OK, and he seems to mean it. Áine goes around to the back of the shed where he prefers to eat, away from the others. It's all she can do not to break into a run, but she doesn't want to draw attention to herself.

As she rounds the corner she spots them: Carlos in his customary spot, a barrel serving as a make-shift table, a crate for a stool, and Madam Daisy, perched up on another crate, sharing ably in his lunch. She takes a moment to steady her breathing, then she strolls over and kisses Daisy on the top of the head.

—I hope she's not being a nuisance.

Carlos shakes his head.

—What have you got there, Missy? she asks Daisy.

—Carlos bringed me my own taco, Daisy says proudly. We were podding peas. Like . . . She puts her finger into her mouth and pulls it out, trying to make a pop. Like . . . She tries again. Carlos says something to her in Spanish, and she tries for a third time. *POP!* Áine only half registers that Daisy seems to have understood the Spanish.

—Very good, Daisy, she says.

She's unsure what to do next. Her instinct is to gather up her daughter in her arms and run out of there, and to keep running all the way to O'Hare. But that would alert Joe, who whether innocent or guilty of . . . something . . . well, he'd be furious either way. He's too unpredictable. Not to mention that O'Hare is over an hour's drive, and that their passports are still in his safe. She doesn't want to frighten Daisy, either. She needs some time. She needs to think.

—Carlos, I need you to take care of Daisy. Please.

He nods.

—Take very good care? She needs to be sure he understands.

—Very good care, he repeats, nodding.

—Don't . . . She's not sure how far to go. Her eyes turn towards the house. Don't . . . Do not let her out of your sight.

He looks directly where she's looking, then back at Áine. She knows he has understood.

—I will bring her in the hoophouse. She stay with me there.

Áine has grateful tears in her eyes when she turns back to the house. Daisy is safe. For now. She needs to get her thoughts straight, let the information settle. She needs some kind of plan. Thankfully, there's still no sign of Joe, but she is expecting him at any minute. Her guts are raw with nerves. She doesn't want him suspecting anything, so she grabs a brush and starts to sweep dust off the porch. Board by board, she starts from the wall of the house with short, firm movements and brushes dust and debris to the edge, and off the porch.

Board by board, she enumerates the facts. Joe has a hidden laptop where he looks at pictures of little girls. Joe grows marijuana, to sell. To pay for his farm, he says. Joe loves his farm, he says. He has fantasies of a wholesome life. A woman around the house, kids running around the farm, a normal life, he says. What he thinks is a normal life. Áine sweeps even harder. Normal? Generations ago, maybe. Or if you're a mail-order bride. That's it, the domestic version of a wwoofer! Joe is a manipulative bastard.

Her sweeping is so vigorous she half-expects to see sparks fly. In the full heat of the day the whole damn place – dry, wooden, a hundred years old – would go up in one big blaze, and good riddance. She imagines the flames licking their way through the stairs, under the floor of the closet in Joe's room, melting the laptop and the cable, burning up the photos, the books. She sees them turning to ash, fluttering up to the attic and the bats.

She's sweltering, from all the sweeping and this blasted heat. Her hair is stuck to her head. She wipes her forehead with the back of her hand and it comes away streaked with dirt. The cloud of dust she raised is settling around her when she realises she has come to a dead stop.

The books. She never thought of checking the yearbook for that woman they met back in May, when they were clearing up after the market. She tries to remember her name. Something Italian. DeLorean, like the car . . . No, Delorente. Vicky Delorente. That was it.

She can't believe that when she met Vicky that day, she was actually jealous. Joe is no one's catch. Maeve could've told her. Her mother could've told her. Probably Vicky Delorente could've told her. But she wouldn't have listened. She would have told them they were wrong, insisted there was chemistry. There is chemistry, there's no denying that. But more and more it's been turning into — she looks at the broom as if she's seeing it for the first time — this.

She spots Joe, coming out of the shed and towards the house.

—Doing some sweeping, Áine, he says as he passes, with a nod of approval.

She pushes a damp strand of hair behind her ear and forces herself to smile until the screen door closes behind him. Somehow she knows that Vicky Delorente holds the missing piece, the piece she needs to end the whole chapter, the whole damn book of Joe. She has to find Vicky and talk to her, but she'll have to figure out how to do it without arousing his suspicions. In the meantime— She lays the brush carefully against the side of the house. She's been through a lot, these past few years, herself and Daisy both, and she's not doing this a moment longer.

He looks her up and down when she comes in.

—Looking hot under the collar there, Áine.

—Farm work is never done, she says, and smiles sweetly.

—What do you say we take the afternoon off, take Daisy, go down to the river?

It was if he read her mind as he went past while she was sweeping. The little woman has had enough. Let's give her an outing.

As long as that was all he read.

—Sounds great, she says.

She takes deep breaths and stays under as long as she can, the cool, green water a balm to her overwrought mind and overheated skin. They might be any normal family, splashing about under the shade of the alder trees. That's when he springs his *surprise*.

—What do you say, Daze? Are you ready to run the show yet?

—What? Daisy says.

—Pardon, corrects Áine automatically, emerging from her watery cloister in time to hear. What? she turns to Joe.

—Want to be Uncle Joe's little helper tomorrow? he asks Daisy, ignoring Áine.

L'il helper.

—At the market? Daisy and Áine ask, in unison.

—Yep. Lincoln Park. The Big City. Rick can't do it tomorrow, so I thought I'd do it myself, take l'il Miss Daze. Been saving it as a surprise.

Every word is a rivet that strikes terror into Áine's heart. *L'il, Daze, surprise.* Tack, tack, tack. She swallows a huge gulp of air, and her knee-jerk outrage with it, and goes under. It's the only way she can think. She has her eyes open, and does not for a moment lose sight of Daisy's sturdy little legs and the frill of her pink swimsuit, and Joe's larger, shadowier ones, further away. Don't let him think you're worried. Maybe there's nothing to be worried about. But maybe there is. She just doesn't know. Now he wants Daisy with him, alone all the way to Chicago, all day at the market. OK, there will be plenty of people there. But alone in the van . . . She thinks again of the pretty little girls on his computer. Shit shit shit. With her thoughts, she releases a stream of bubbles through her nose. She needs to buy time. She'll let him think it's a great idea, then she'll find a reason to go herself at the last minute. But then what? As her air runs out her thoughts run amok. How much time does she have? What are her options?

She explodes to the surface, gasping.

—Mummy, Mummy, we thought you were never coming up.

Joe only raises his eyebrows. As if to say, we thought it, and we did nothing about it. As if to say, and what have you got to say about that? Don't be an idiot, she tells herself. You're letting your imagination run away with you.

—Well? he says. What do you say, *Mummy*?

It takes a moment to realise he's talking about Daisy going to the market, not about her drowning. Nor is he really asking a question. It's more like a test, and she's hesitated a moment too long.

—You don't trust me to take her, huh? He looks at her with narrowed eyes. As if he can sense the conclusions she's coming to about him. As if he knows he's running out of time. Or is he just offended? He's been host to them for three weeks. Not the greatest host, that's for sure, but he's tried, in his way. He's taking time out to take them to the river right now. And he's always patient with Daisy. But there's no damn way she's sending her five-year-old off in a van with some guy she barely knows. And one she doesn't feel very good about, now she's seen his weed, and his *l'il cuties*. She feigns the water irritating her eyes and rubs at them.

—Um, I don't know . . . What do you say, Daisy?

There was the long shot that she wouldn't want to go. She never chose to spend time with Joe, always

153

preferring to potter around the house with Áine, or to watch Carlos. She seems to be a bit afraid of him. Maybe she can sense something. Or maybe it's from the time he wanted to bring her up to see the bats. But the fact is, as much as Daisy loves trailing around the farm after Carlos, she has been asking if they can go shopping, or to a playground. She's missing the city, and friends her own age.

—Will you come too, Mummy? Let's go, let's go. Please! We can go to the Mall.

She's jumping and splashing water everywhere. Áine takes in Joe's scowl. It could be that he's being thwarted in something, or it could simply be that he doesn't like malls. All that silliness and wasting money.

Then the plan that had so far eluded her cements into place. The perfect opportunity, and she nearly missed it.

—I'll come for the ride, she tells Joe calmly, but I'd really like some time to myself.

Another time, this would have been out of the question. She was there to work, he'd remind her gently. Farm work is never done, Áine, he might add. There's no doubt, the spell of Joe is well and truly broken.

—Fine, he snaps.

They load up the van in the small hours, packing it tightly with stacked crates of produce – the heirlooms, the peppers, the basils and the rest – until it smells like the essence of nature itself, all damp and earthy and cool. It fills Áine with a longing that goes back to her childhood, growing up on the farm; that might go all the way back to the garden of Eden, for all she knows. Complete with snake. Joe goes inside to get the cash box from the safe, and she follows him in to get Daisy. She's left her asleep until the last minute. As she's passing his bedroom, she sees the door of the safe swinging wide open, sees Joe lift out the green metal box, and sees, there, neat at the back, their burgundy Irish passports. She steps quietly in, and comes close enough that she only has to reach in. Would he stop her? On what grounds? Would she ruin the plan she's hatched? She is not completely confident that she can stop her arm from moving, past Joe's shoulder into the cool, dark safe. Everything hinges on this moment, or so it seems. He must feel it too, because he turns and meets her eye, and follows it to where it rests on the passports. With a small, inward-looking smile he closes the heavy door.

She draws in a sharp breath, and tells him she's going to wake Daisy.

They pull out once Daisy is tucked into her seat with a blanket to ward off the cool morning air. It's only beginning to get light when they start to see an occasional warehouse or storage facility in Chicago's furthest reaches.

—Gas, Joe says, the first words he's spoken, as he pulls into a Shell.

As soon as he goes in to the store to pay, she whips out her phone. She's had it charging all night. She hardly slept all night, in fact. She left Joe ensconced in Tour de France highlights and went back to Daisy where, under the covers, she started her frantic online search for Vicky Delorente, and Victoria Delorente, and Vicky De Lorente, and every permutation she could think of. She sent a group email to every single Vicky or Victoria she could find in the state of Illinois: *Hi Vicky, met you in May in Lincoln Park, with Joe Martello. Need to talk. Can you meet? In Chicago in the morn. Urgent.* She's been checking her in-box constantly ever since. A few of the Vickys bounced back. One wrote to say she'd got the wrong person. She checks again: no new mail. Joe is walking back to the van so she puts the phone away quickly.

—So, what are you going to do with this *time?* he asks as he pulls back into traffic. He's unable to keep the sarcasm out of his voice.

Good question. A manicure, maybe a facial, she thinks of saying, imagining how furious that would make him. He hates frivolous women. For some reason, she thinks of Vicky Delorente and her perky voice. She can easily imagine her spending her Saturdays on manicures and facials.

—I was thinking of taking a look around the

market, sussing out the competition, she says instead, knowing it's nothing that'd particularly appeal to Daisy. And showing an interest in the farm too, that'd throw him. He was a sucker for the good worker.

—Then maybe take a walk around Lincoln Park, she adds. But first, I'll help set up, of course.

He looks at her suspiciously. She'll have to tone it down a bit.

They set up the stand, and unload and arrange all the produce. Áine hasn't been back here since May, and it feels like a lifetime ago. One or two of the other traders come over to say hello. One of them, the woman who sells flowers, pats Daisy on the head.

—Want to come see my stall?

—Great, Áine answers for them both without looking at Joe, and walks to the other side of the trestle tables. Might just take a stroll while we're at it, she calls back.

The woman, Kim, must be bored, because she wants to tell Daisy the names of every single flower. Áine takes a discreet look at her phone. At last. *Hi Aine, I remember you. With Joe. I can meet. Can you find the Blarney Stone?* She gives the address and a phone number, with instructions to ring or text any time, that she's on her way there herself. It strikes Áine as an odd place for an American woman to choose to meet, in the morning especially, though she had mentioned it before, and there was the Irish boyfriend. For Áine's purposes, it's as good a place as any. *On my way*, she taps into her phone. They will take a taxi.

—Come on, Daisy. Let's go see if we can find a playground. Maybe you could tell Joe we'll be back before lunch? she says to Kim.

—Sure. Oh, the playground, it's over— but Áine has grabbed Daisy's hand and they are already on their way.

They get there in under thirty minutes, thanks to Sunday-morning traffic. It's a drab-looking bar, exactly what she expected; badly in need of a paint job, the broken neon sign incongruous with its heritage namesake. It doesn't even look open, which is not surprising since it's not yet ten. But when she tries the door, it yields.

—Eew. Daisy holds her nose.

It stinks of stale beer and smoke and disinfectant. It occurs to Áine that maybe children aren't allowed into bars here. Well, they can always go somewhere else, once she's found Vicky. At first glance, there does not seem to be anybody around, but her eyes adjust to the murky light and she's able to make out a dark figure seated at the bar, a bottle of stout and a glass of amber liquid in front of him. Ten o'clock. Her heart sinks. He is exactly the kind of customer she imagined in a place called the Blarney Stone.

—Hello? she calls.

He lifts his head.

—I'm looking for Vicky, Vicky Delorente?

—There's just meself here, he says, with a strong Irish midlands accent. And John. That's the barman.

On cue, a dark, curly head appears up from a hole in the floor behind the bar, attached to a well-built man in his mid-thirties, or thereabouts.

—Who's taking my name in vain? he asks.

—I'm looking for someone called Vicky Delorente.

—And who should I say is asking? He winks at her.

Jesus. Áine knows his kind. He's probably spent years honing his Sam Malone banter, and she's not in the mood.

—A friend, she says shortly.

—And what about you, little lady. Are you as grumpy as your mammy this morning?

Before Daisy can answer, the door opens, briefly admitting a shaft of morning light into the dingy bar. It's Vicky. Áine is so relieved to see her that she rushes over and hugs her, not something she usually does to strangers.

—Thank you so much for meeting me. I really need to talk to you. It's about . . .

She looks at Daisy. She hadn't thought about what she would do with Daisy. She doesn't want her overhearing.

Vicky has noticed Daisy too, and she looks alarmed. It doesn't reassure Áine to see the way Vicky is struggling to control her reaction.

—Are you guys *staying* with Joe? Both of you?

Áine nods. She sees Vicky's involuntary shudder. But then Vicky recovers herself.

—Let's get you some coffee and we can talk. John, she calls. Can you set . . . What's your name, sweetie?

—Daisy.

—Cute name. Do you like foosball? She points to the table at the other end of the room. Daisy shrugs. Come on. It's a lot of fun. John is pretty good at it. Not as good as me. But pretty good. Think you could beat him?

John ambles out from behind the bar good-naturedly. There's something in the glance between them, something understated and real, which Áine realises with a pang is something she's never known. Not with Conor, not even in the early days, and certainly not with Joe. And that it's probably what she's come all the way here to find, dragging Daisy with her.

—Is there coffee on? Vicky asks him.

—Specially for you, he replies, brushing her hand as he goes past.

Áine feels teary at the futility of it, and the trouble she might have caused by thinking she has some right to this kind of connection with another human being.

Vicky goes behind the bar and comes back with two mugs of freshly brewed coffee. Áine accepts hers gratefully and takes a swallow, willing the hot brew to bring her back into focus. There's no delicate way to put it, no smooth segue, so she takes a deep breath and asks outright.

—Why did Joe drop out of teacher-training?

Vicky looks to where Daisy is slamming and spinning the rods like crazy and her boyfriend is pretending to struggle to keep up. She bites on her lip, as if she's trying to choose her words.

—Truth is, I don't know for sure.

Áine waits. The clatter and slam of the foosball fades out as Vicky tells her story.

It was so long ago. They were friends, not even close friends. They hung out together between classes sometimes, that was about it. Joseph was really interesting, and talented. He'd been some kind of prodigy when he was a kid. And he was super smart. Nothing was hard for him. Oftentimes, he challenged other students and professors with his fast, compelling arguments, and all of this set him apart. She used to try to persuade him to tone it down, but it was like he couldn't stop himself. Not that it mattered. He had a perfect record, straight As, right up until . . .

On the table in front of her, Vicky's untouched coffee is going cold. Áine can see this is a story Vicky has to tell, one she's been wanting to tell for a long time, but she wants her to hurry up and get to the point.

—What happened?

Vicky continues as if she hasn't heard.

—It was kind of . . . I mean, it was my fault, Joe leaving. Something he said. It was nothing really . . .

Áine's guts are contracting with the tension. She needs the toilet, but she needs to stay and hear. At the same time, she doesn't know if she can bear to hear. She forces herself to let Vicky continue.

They had to go on placements before they could get their teaching licences. She got the first graders she was hoping for. Joe applied for fourth grade but he got second instead. They got stuck in and they were both super busy, so they didn't see much of each other all semester. Plus, their schools were at opposite sides of the city.

It was the last day of her placement when she bumped into him on campus. A Friday. She was on her way to the department office, wanting to drop off her report before the weekend, and they met in the stairwell. He started talking real fast, that way he does, about all kinds of random stuff. She only caught snatches, but he seemed to want to get something off his chest, so when he asked if she wanted to go for a beer, she agreed.

They went to the student bar. It was still pretty

early, so there weren't many people about. Joe was smoking weed and he sculled a couple of beers real fast. She had barely touched hers when he was ordering his third, and then his fourth. She was worried he might be having a crisis about teaching, that after getting all this way to the end of the course he'd changed his mind. She'd heard it happen, students who were super keen in lectures, falling apart when they went into an actual classroom. It was understandable. Kids can be a real handful, especially at that age.

—But then you know that, she says, as if she's only just remembering Áine is here. I'm sorry. It's kind of hard to talk about, even though I've been expecting someone to ask me about it for . . . well, since it happened. I want you to know exactly what . . . how . . . I mean, I never knew for sure if what I did was the right thing.

Joe talked and talked. He drank more beers. He told her about the kids, and all the songs they'd learned. He was totally musical. Just picked up a guitar and he knew how to play it. Same with just about any instrument. He had them playing triangles and tambourines and maracas, their own little band, marching around the playground. Sounded like he'd had just about the best placement experience ever. The kids too. He was gonna ace the course, pick up any job he wanted. And he was perfect for it. That's the thing. He'd have made a great teacher. If she hadn't . . . If he hadn't said what he said.

Áine felt for this woman. She was clearly distressed by her story, but she didn't have time for sympathy.

—What is it, Vicky, what did Joe say?

Vicky took a deep breath and came out with it.

—He said he was glad he got second graders after all, that the ten-year-olds were too . . . That he couldn't concentrate around them because they were too distracting, that the six-year-olds were bad enough.

—Jesus.

Áine lets it sink in. It's bad. Yet not as bad as she expected . . . It could still have all been overreaction, jumping to conclusions when she realised Joe wasn't going to give her what she wanted, and she was looking for excuses to get away.

But Vicky hasn't finished.

She didn't register what he'd said at first. Probably because it was such a shock; it was not what you wanted to hear some guy, your friend, say. And because he was talking about all kinds of stuff, it kind of got lost in the middle. One minute it was about the kids riffing to the Dead, then it was all about his dad, next thing he was talking about this German class he'd taken, how it turned out he was fluent. Crazy stuff. I mean, how could someone be fluent in a language after one semester? So she thought she must've heard wrong. But the words wormed their way into recognition in spite of their haphazard delivery, and she couldn't let it pass, as much as she wanted to. She tried to ask him about it, but he gave her a funny look and just kept on talking. She had to put her hand on his arm to still the flow. She asked, What did he mean, distracting? He laughed first, said he was kidding. But then his face changed. He got angry, shook her hand off, said that it was bullshit pretending kids are totally asexual, said he could totally buy that Humbert Humbert guy who was into nymphets, young girls. He said fourth graders were a bunch of little Lolitas.

When he saw the way she was looking at him, and moving back from him in her seat, he laughed, said she needn't worry, it wasn't for him, he was just saying he could see why some guys took it further, that was all.

She finished up her beer and left as soon as she could. She wanted to believe him when he said he was kidding, but she was in a total state. She couldn't eat, couldn't concentrate for days, trying to figure out the right thing to do. It was no small accusation, if she did accuse him of . . . something. He would never be able to teach. Could she have that on her conscience, just because of some drunken rant? In the end she went with her gut and told the Dean what had happened, and the next day Joe was gone.

Just like that. She never found out what happened, and she didn't see Joe again until that time at the farmers' market, back in May.

—I had to act like he was an old friend that time . . . I mean, I'm pretty sure he knows it was because of me, but . . .

Vicky stops. She puts her hand to her mouth. She's looking down towards Daisy.

—He hasn't . . . Tell me he hasn't.

Áine shakes her head firmly.

—Oh my god, that's such a relief. When I got your mail I didn't know what to think. I didn't know you had a daughter, that she was there, with Joe. So, what was it that made you contact me?

Áine tells her about the hidden laptop. She takes out her phone and shows her *l'il cuties*.

—It's the same sort of thing. Not terrible, but you know it is terrible anyway, you just can't put your finger on it.

Vicky nods.

—Exactly. I've been afraid something like this . . . For so long. She takes both of Áine's hands. I completely understand if you want to just get away, take Daisy and get out of here as fast as you can. But what if . . .

The *what if* hangs between them like an undetonated bomb, and Áine has flashes of *l'il cuties* in the attic, in the barn, in the basement.

—Should we call the cops? Vicky asks at last, echoing her own thoughts.

—I don't want to be there, I don't want Daisy seeing that. I don't know there's anything to report, really . . .

Vicky nods.

—That's the way it was for me too. But you don't want to stay, right?

Áine definitely does not want to stay. Maybe she is over-reacting, but she doesn't want to be around Joe a moment longer than she has to be. The adventure is over, and Daisy was right, it was nothing like Dora's. What she was looking for isn't here. She wants to go home. To Maeve, to her mother, to the life she took for granted before.

—You could stay with me, call the cops from there?

—I need to go back to the farm, Áine says. Our passports are there. I wasn't able to bring them with me. She thinks about the key of the safe, on the bulging keyring that Joe keeps in the knee pocket of his shorts.

—The cops would take care of that.

—I'm not sure. I mean, maybe there's nothing illegal . . .

What if Joe was completely innocent? She didn't want to get caught up in a mess like that. She just wanted to go home.

—OK, I understand. Can you drive? Take his car.

—I'd be terrified he'd follow. Or that I'd get lost.

—Where does he live?

Áine names the town. Vicky nods.

—I'd have to get the keys.

—Take his keys when he's asleep. He has to sleep sometime, surely. Leave early, get out onto the 90. Pull over when you get near the city and call me. I'll pick you guys up, take you back with me. Or to the airport. Wherever you want.

—Tomorrow?

—Tomorrow, Vicky confirms. And the cops – I'll let you decide. Just get away from Joe.

She expects Joe to be annoyed when they get back to the market, but he is busy with customers and she decides, from a distance, to deposit Daisy at the flower stall so she won't give anything away about Vicky. She's been warned, and bribed, but there's still a chance she'll blurt something out. By the time he notices she's back, she is busy herself, giving an elderly couple a pitch about spinach that could have earned her an academy award.

—You done with your *time*? he asks when the couple leave, laden with produce.

—Mm hm, she says lightly. Want to go take a break yourself?

It goes better than she expected.

—I'm good. He stops, looks at her thoughtfully. But thank you. Thank you, Áine.

—K, she replies, trying not to let his sudden gratitude faze her. I'll just sort this lot. She indicates the confusion of heirloom tomatoes. Then we're almost out.

She collects Daisy when they're leaving, and to Áine's relief she promptly falls asleep as soon as the van starts up, tired out from her early start.

They're out on the open road when Joe turns to her, his expression serious.

—I appreciate your help, Áine.

—Sure, she says.

—No, I mean, I really appreciate your help. Yours and Daisy's. He glances in Daisy's direction. When she hasn't changed teams, that is.

He grins. Áine stiffens, then realises he means Kim at the flower stall.

—See, he continues. See, it's not often I get to be part, really part, of a team, Awn. And I think we make a pretty good team. It can get super lonely, out on the farm. In the winter, especially. I'm sure going to miss you guys when you leave.

—We'll miss you too, Áine lies. But he's already lost in his own thoughts of the approaching Chicago winter.

Áine puts Daisy to bed after a late dinner, then goes to join Joe in his den where he's busy laying his

169

leaves out on cigarette papers and interspersing them with buds. His keyring is to one side, to make sitting more comfortable. Áine eyes them, trying to decide which one fits the safe. She doesn't need to worry about the car key anymore; while Joe was out checking his plants, she went on a frantic rummage in all the drawers and nooks and crannies she could think of, before inspiration struck and she checked the glove compartment of the car. There it was – the spare key. He rolls up and lights up, and soon he's enfolded in a world of permeable boundaries and infinite possibilities, interesting only to himself.

—Just going to check on Daisy, Áine says when she's sure he has dozed off. When he doesn't respond she carefully lifts the keyring and goes to their room. There, she extricates three of the most likely candidates, then tiptoes back to the den and replaces the ring. Back in their room, she quickly gathers up their things into two carry-on bags. Next, she goes to the bathroom and stuffs a full toilet roll into the toilet, then flushes so the water rises all the way to the top. She checks on Joe once more before going to the safe. She succeeds on the first try. Once the passports are safely tucked into her bag, she gets into bed.

With every minute that passes, Áine tries to persuade herself that the dark has grown a shade lighter, that dawn is nearly here. If she slept at all, it was in short, unrestful bouts, every time startling back to wakefulness. Beside her, where she lies fully clothed under a sheet, are the two small bags containing all Daisy's belongings and her own few essentials. She'll carry these downstairs and put them into the car. The car door is already ajar, and the spare key is in the ignition. Then she'll come back up and carry Daisy down. If Joe wakes – though he's a heavy sleeper – she'll say she's taking Daisy to the toilet. The downstairs toilet, because the upstairs one is blocked. She should have crashed with exhaustion, but she's too charged with adrenaline. Up since four yesterday. Or was it today? Already the Blarney Stone and Vicky seem so far away.

At last she's able to make out shapes in the room. She eases herself up soundlessly and moves to the window. When she opens the shutter a crack, it is to the blue-grey light of dawn; it's time. She takes the two bags and moves soundlessly to the door, light-headed with terror. Every step in the creaky old house is potentially the one that will wake Joe. He's a heavy sleeper, she tells herself again, and keeps on putting one foot in front of the other, one step on the stairs after the other, until the bags are deposited on the back seat of the car.

Now Daisy.

She creeps upstairs again. This is riskier. Daisy

might make some noise. She will have to move fast. She slides a hand under Daisy's knees, another under her armpits, and before she has even opened her eyes, or her mouth to ask a sleepy *what's happening?*, Áine is already down the stairs and half way out the back door. She can hardly believe she has got this far.

But then she hears it, a car, coming up the driveway.

In her panic she cannot think of a way to explain why she has her sleeping child in her arms at this hour. All she is thinking is that the noise will wake Joe before she can get away. Then the ancient Taurus that Carlos drives comes around the corner. Of course. She had forgotten how early Carlos started. Joe hates that he's always here before he's even awake. Makes him look bad. What will she say? Should she just keep going, dump Daisy into the back of Joe's car and drive out past him, steal his boss's car right in front of him?

Carlos reaches the house just as she gets to Joe's car. He takes in the scene in a single glance, then he turns in the direction of the top window, Joe's den, before he gives the slightest shake of his head. Áine hesitates. Has he seen something? Is Joe up?

Carlos jumps out and holds open the back door of his car.

—In here.

In a moment he has taken Daisy out of her arms

172

and put her onto the back seat. His eyes meet Áine's, and she sees what his actions mean, what it means for his family. There will be no coming back after this. But she also sees that he is helping her because when he looks at Daisy he is thinking of his daughters, of Rosa who used to follow him around everywhere.

—The bags . . .

She runs to Joe's car and snatches the bags, then she jumps into the front beside Carlos. The engine is still running. Carlos puts his foot down and swings the car around. As they speed down the driveway he points to the rear-view mirror. Áine turns. The last thing she sees as they turn onto the road is Joe, coming to a halt in his front yard, an expression of complete bewilderment on his face.

Daisy

Carlos's car is old and noisy. When you . . . *cover your ears* . . . it makes no difference. It's worse than Joe's. Joe's has bottles and cans and shells from sunflower seeds. Your feet crunch on them when you're getting in and out. Joe is able to take the shells off with just his teeth and his tongue. He spits the shells out onto the floor. It's yukky but Mummy says not to say so because everyone is different and it would be rude. Mummy is afraid of Joe getting cross.

Daddy is never cross. When he picks me up from school on Fridays he hugs and hugs me and tells me he misses me. Sometimes Daddy brings me to school, but he doesn't live near school any more. He lives in a partment. I like seeing Daddy, but I don't like his partment. It's boring. He hasn't even got a TV, only his computer. He's always watching shows on his computer. Joe's farm is not boring. There's cats. But they run away when I try to play with them. I am practising staying quiet so I can pet one. Carlos says their kittens get borned in Joe's stove. The stove doesn't work. That's good, because then the kittens would be burnded.

Carlos doesn't talk much. He's not talking now either, he's just driving. I don't know where we're going. Maybe we're not going back to Joe's farm and I'll never see the kittens getting borned in the stove. Thinking about the kittens makes me sad. I wish I had Mr Snuggly.

Joe is scary when he talks fast. Sometimes he wants me to do things I don't want to do. I pretend the bats are not there, even though they are because I saw them. Joe says they are not bad like bampires the way everyone thinks. He says they poop out fruit seeds and that's good. I don't care if their poop has seeds, it's stinky. It stinked my dress. Mummy gets cross when I tell her it's still stinky.

Mummy forgot to strap me. The guards will stop Carlos and put him in jail because he forgot to strap me.

—Mummy and Carlos you forgot to strap me!

Carlos says something to Mummy, and Mummy turns around. She looks like she forgot I was here. I tell her again she forgot to strap me. She leans into the back seat to find the seat belt. She is feeling around for it, but she's looking out the back window. I start to kneel so I can look out the back window too and Mummy says *Sit down*. I don't know why she's cross. Mummy pats me on the head and says *Sorry sweetie, sorry honeybunch*. She finds the seat belt where it was stuck down the back of the seat. It's all old and dusty but she puts it on me anyway. Then Mummy finds my Dora backpack. It was on the floor beside me and I never knowed. I'm happy now, because when I open the zip I see Mr Snuggly and all my stuff.

Maybe we're going home and I'll see Daddy and Daddy will bring me to the Big Blue Barn for a play. We won't be going up the big mountain though. That makes me feel sad again. I wanted to go camping up the big mountain. Maybe I can go camping with Daddy. That would be better than staying in Daddy's boring old partment. I'll ask Daddy to bring me camping. His new friend Lucy can come too.

Lucy sometimes buys me things. *Say thank you to Lucy, Daze*. Mummy gets mad when Lucy buys me new clothes. I don't think I should say thank you to Lucy because I don't want her to buy me clothes. Sometimes the clothes are nice. Sweets are better. I can eat them up before I go home to Mummy.

Daddy is different when Lucy is there. I think Daddy will marry Lucy. If Daddy marries Lucy I want a very pretty dress and to be a flower girl. Mummy can't be cross if I'm a flower girl. I might go and live with Daddy and Lucy because they'll be the Mummy and Daddy. I'll miss Mummy then instead of Daddy. Daddy will need a new house because I have lots of toys. I hope it will have a TV. I hope it will not have bats.

Frank

——W hat the . . . ? Goddam. Learn how to drive, asshole. Goddam immigrants.

Frank swerves the Cadillac expertly and narrowly misses the old Taurus. His heart is racing.

—Did you see that, Judy? Right into our lane. If I hadn't . . .

He glances at his wife. She's swallowing and blinking her way out of sleep at the commotion he's making. Missed the whole thing. He feels a rare burst of pity for her. Better the world she was in when she was asleep. How disappointed she always looks once she feels her way into her over-sized body, once she creaks her joints awake and takes a cautious, wheezy breath.

But he's the one who has to live with it, with all

178

this disappointment, and she's been disappointed just about their whole life together. His self-pity hardens into the more comfortable emotion, low-grade anger. There's always something missing for Judy. Don't matter what he gives her, it's never enough. She doesn't say, but he can tell. She never thought he was good enough. Never mind that she was nothing but a shop-girl. He was doing her a favour. Who the hell did she think she was? And now . . .

—Sorry, Frank, I must've nodded off, Judy says through a yawn. You sure wanted to leave good and early.

—Miss traffic, Frank says curtly. But he's also remembering her slow shuffle to the driveway in the dark, the manoeuvring it took to wedge her huge behind in the door and onto the passenger seat, the effort to swing her legs in. He's ashamed that even at that hour he was glancing around to make sure no one was watching. Her rasping breath, her apologies, changing her mind. *No, I'll stay, Frank. You go on ahead.* Only he couldn't face going through the whole routine in reverse. Then the too short seat belt . . . The tightening in his chest . . .

Judy's weight embarrasses Frank. Embarrasses him, and makes him angry. It's like she did it to him, personally. He tries to stay out of the house. She says *You work too hard, Frank. You should retire.* He tells her he wants to be sure they have enough put by in the pension fund, even though they already have enough in the bank to cruise the world for the rest of their days and still leave a couple of million for Joe. Besides, what's he gonna do, manoeuvring round the bulk of Judy in the house all day? There's another reason, too. A tiny, foolish part of him keeps hoping that if he hangs in there long enough, instead of selling up he'll be able to pass the business on: *Frank Martello & Son.*

But there's the heart thing. How long can he afford to wait? He's been having chest pains for a few months now. His doctor has booked him in for a by-pass in a couple of weeks and he still hasn't told Judy. Truth is, he's more worried about her heart than his, with all that weight she's carrying. He doesn't want her worrying. And it is a worry. Her heart, his heart. A thing like that changes a man. Puts things in perspective. Things like Joe. Fact is, Joe's the only thing that makes Judy happy. It's not like Frank didn't know this all along. A shrink – Frank's a Sopranos fan – would probably tell him he was always jealous of Joe, the way Judy was so caught up in that kid. It's just since his chest he started to think he should do something positive, like bringing Judy out finally to visit Joe's farm.

Farm. That's a joke. Frank knows business. Don't matter if it's cars, or encyclopedias, or vegetables. And this ain't no business. A glance at the books –

another joke – is all it takes. Well, today Frank's taking care of business. He's thinking he'll waive Joe's loan. That way he can play at farms without doing any harm. And if that don't make Judy happy, he doesn't know what will. She's been wanting to come out here long enough, that's for sure. Frank just hopes that seeing Joe will make up for the rest of the so-called farm.

—Too bad I missed out on the pretty scenery, huh?

—You didn't miss nothing. It was dark most of the time. Besides, what's there to see, corn? He waves an arm around the flat farmland, still grainy in the pre-dawn light.

Judy gives a little sigh that could mean anything.

—I sure hope the dogs are doing OK . . .

Frank hates the sight of the dogs, hates their incessant barking, the way she lets them piss all over the house. She's bringing them up now to antagonise him. Well, it's working. The muscles of his chest harden again, and it hurts when he turns the wheel into the lane that leads to Joe's farm.

Light is only breaking, but there's Joe, standing in the driveway outside the house. Judy stirs in her seat, tugs at her dress where it's settled into her fleshy folds.

—Look, there he is! So early!

For a second Frank's impressed too. Joe talked

181

enough about getting to the markets but he'd never really believed it. He'd expected to have to shuffle around the farmyard with Judy for an hour or so, but maybe he'd been wronging him. Maybe Joe really was making a go of things. There's that flicker of hope again. *& Son.* But it doesn't take long for him to see that something is not right. Joe looks like he can't decide whether he's coming or going. What the hell is going on? Is he drunk or what? So much for surprising him. Judy's idea, of course.

—So much for surprising him, he says sourly.

—What's he doing?

Frank can size up a customer at a hundred yards, knows their hopes, dreams, and bank balance before they're even properly in focus. Sends them home in something different to what they had in mind, convinced, as they climb into the car with heated seats, or leather trim, or an extra couple of hundred cc, that they just moved up the food-chain. One look at Joseph is enough to tell him that the best thing they could do right now would be to drive past their son, turn around in the yard, and drive straight back out again.

But you can't push back a clock. Frank doesn't know where he'd push it to anyhow. You can't put a grown man back into his mother and forget he ever happened. He's here. They're here. He's going to have to put up with whatever Joe's bullshit story is this time.

He hits the brakes. The hood dips just inches away from Joe. He turns the key. Judy's *Ohmygod Frank, you're going to hit him!* breaks shrilly into sudden silence. Joe jumps back, but his reaction is delayed, off by several seconds. Up close, Frank watches, fascinated, as Joe struggles to control his crazed expression. As he looks first at his mother, then at Frank, his expression transforms to disbelief.

There's this pause, like time has stopped, watching Joe watching them, and Frank wants Joe's discomfort to last as long as possible. But then he remembers. The heart thing. His decision. Reluctantly he breaks eye contact with Joe, takes a deep breath and turns to Judy.

—Let's go inside.

Joe is already at the passenger door when Frank gets there to help Judy.

—Dad. Mom. What a crazy surprise. Let's . . . um . . . take a walk. See the new hoophouse. It's super close to finished.

He's talking the whole time. Frank tells himself to breathe. That's what the doctor told him. Slow, deep breaths. Don't do anything stressful. When Joe sees his mother her size takes his words away, at least for a moment. Then he starts up again, talking, talking, talking, like a goddam wind-up toy.

—OK. Let's see here. What have we got? So we

got to . . . OK. Let's get this leg over here. OK. No, not going to work. Maybe, how about . . . ?

—How about you go inside, tidy up? I'll help your mother. Make some coffee.

—Gotcha. Jeez, Dad, I wasn't expecting . . .

Frank ignores him and sets about hauling Judy out of the seat. No heavy lifting, the doctor told him. He manages to get her turned, both feet on the ground, then he puts his arms under hers and bends his knees.

—On three . . . he gasps, and with a wet sucking sound of the leather parting company with her thighs, she's up.

—O my, Judy says.

—O my is right, Frank says. He puts an arm around her, as far as it will go, and together they make their way slowly to the house.

—O my, Judy says again once they're inside. She's looking around with an expression that wants to be delighted but can only manage dismay. She hasn't been in Joe's house before. It is a shock, the first time. Maybe it's not as bad as Frank's seen it in the past – the overflowing trash, the take-out cartons and coffee cups across every surface, the smell – but it's still pretty bad. Maybe – Frank doesn't like to admit it, but maybe he wanted to shock Judy, let her see exactly how her precious son lives.

He gets her into the kitchen, where there's no sign

of Joe, no sign of coffee, and guides her to the most solid-looking chair. After giving it a trial shake for sturdiness he wipes it with his elbow and sits her down. He goes to the hall and calls up the stairs.

—Joe?

There's silence.

—Joseph!

After a pause there are footsteps, and Joe appears at the top of the stairs.

—Be right there, sir. Just got to . . .

Frank's patience has run out.

—Just got to nothing. You see your mother, what, maybe twice in the year? You think you could make your mother a coffee? Right now.

He's not shouting.

Joe takes a look towards whatever it is he thinks he's got to do, but he thinks better of it, and comes down. Giving Frank a wide berth, he goes into the kitchen. Frank follows and stands by Judy, who is trying hard not to absorb the fact that her son lives like a squatter. Worse than. He should've warned her better. He's ashamed that he didn't, that maybe he didn't on purpose. He puts a hand on the wadge of flesh that covers her shoulder. A memory comes to him of himself as a small boy, helping his mama to knead the dough for the pizza. But it's not flour and water that's beneath his hand. Buried beneath his wife's warm flesh the tips of his fingers can feel bone. It was her collarbones he noticed when he first saw her, working behind the counter in Mr Grube's shop, and the way her dress fell from them, simple and lovely.

Joe is standing at the sink, holding up a filthy mug that says *Support Lance*. It's shaking in his hand. He's looking around wildly, as if he doesn't know what he's looking for. Still holding the mug, he goes to the refrigerator and opens it. A rancid smell fills the room. Judy turns her head slightly. Frank's made up his mind they're not consuming anything out of that kitchen when Joe produces two beers and puts them triumphantly on the table.

—What about a beer instead, guys? He begins twisting the cap.

The bang of fist hitting formica stops him short.

—Your mother does not drink beer. At this hour of the morning, I do not drink beer. And you can forget the coffee. Your mother cannot sit in this house. My God, Joseph, how can you live like this?

Here he was, starting up exactly like he vowed he would not. *How can you live like this?* Been saying it for twenty years. Ever since Joe quit college like that, out of the blue. Frank didn't give a dime for Joe's college course anyhow. Far as he could see, the boy had a job, a career laid on a plate for him: *Frank Martello & Son*. Thumbed his nose at that. It was good enough to put food on the table, a roof over their heads, to pay the fees to all his fine schools and college, but it was not good enough for Joseph. Embarrasses him, his dream of putting up the new sign. Should've been well disabused of that by now. He convinced himself it was Judy's doing, all that fancy piano she had the kid doing when he was little. God knows Frank did his best, playing catch in the back yard till he was bored dumb, little league every weekend . . . All the good any of it did. Kid had a bad attitude right from the start.

Frank knew Joe was smoking that goddam weed since forever. When he was in his teens, the fights got out of hand. The time he had Joe by the scruff of the neck, up against the wall, Judy begging him to stop. OK, so he was wrong, getting physical like that. And it wasn't like it ever did any good. *If I'd a known you were coming* . . . he's saying now. Like that'd change anything. The goddam weed. It hits Frank suddenly. Is he growing it now? Is that what this secrecy and panicking is all about?

—Your mother wanted to surprise you, he says levelly.

Judy looks up at him. He can't tell if she's glad he's speaking up for her, or if she's reprimanding him, willing him to leave Joe be.

—Guess I'm not good at surprises, Joe says, distracted. He's gone to the doorway again, looking towards the front door. Then another look at the stairs.

—What the hell is so goddam important upstairs?
Eh?

Something occurs to him. Maybe it's nothing to
do with weed. Maybe it's something that would
make it all OK.

—You got a girl up there or something?

He forces himself to smile when he says it, like a
much-too-late father-son offering. But Joe looks so
startled that Frank's sorry he said it, sorry he thought
there might be any normal explanation. There was
never a normal explanation where Joe was concerned.
Never a girlfriend either, as far as Frank knew. A
boyfriend? A sigh releases from somewhere deep
inside him; a long-ago, far-away place.

—We'll go get coffee, he says finally. That place
by the bank, they're 24-hour. I went last time I was
out here.

It comes out monotonous, resigned. Frank has never
seen Joseph look so agitated. He doesn't show any
sign that he's even heard. Has he moved on to hard
drugs or something? That's what they say happens,
once you start with that marijuana.

—Are you listening to me?

Joe's head shoots up.

—Coffee. We'll drive over together, have breakfast together, a family. Do you think you can handle
that?

Judy pipes up.

—That sounds just lovely, Frank. Doesn't it, Joseph? Doesn't it sound lovely?

Frank bends to help her up. He inclines his head to Joe to do the same.

—On three. One . . .

—I'm sorry . . . so much trouble . . . Judy is saying. Joe is grunting at the effort. Frank feels that tightening again. Just get her to her feet. One, two . . .

—There.

They stand, still with their arms around each other, all three catching their breath. Behind the breathing Frank can hear birdsong. Are they always this loud? Behind the birds, there's something else off in the distance, coming closer. Frank is struggling to separate the sounds out, trying to make sense of them, but the pain in his chest is not fading, the way it usually does. A bright light penetrates the grime on the window and spreads slowly, probing the shapes and shadows of the kitchen, flooding the table and the chairs, moving across their shapeless, helpless huddle.

2016

Makiko

Makiko's jagged-edged mountains form a straight, grey line. They should not be straight but she can't help it. No matter what her intention, when she lines her stones up, this is the way they land. Sitting back on her heels, she picks up the small rake and draws it through the gravel. She is not expert. Zen gardening is something she learned while living in Chicago, something a doctor prescribed when she went to seek help for anxiety.

—Research suggests, he said, in his soporific voice, that the subconscious mind is sensitive to a subtle association between the rocks. He then picked up a doll-sized rake from where it lay beside the sandbox on his desk, and began to lose himself in drawing row after row of wavy patterns.

—And that this may be responsible for the calming effect of the garden, he added when he remembered his patient.

Lately she has been spending a lot of time raking.

—This is not a monastery, Makiko, Oba Kikue said when Makiko began marking out the area with bamboo, two metres by two. We are not nuns.

The same Oba who, when Makiko, not a little proudly, announced her engagement to her tall, Western boyfriend, said only

—Marriage is a woman's grave.

Makiko had made the trip from Tokyo to Kyoto especially that day. She wanted to tell her Oba in person because as a child she had always felt she was a favourite of Oba Kikue. She also went because she hoped Oba Kikue would be pleased for her in a way that her mother was not.

—Could you not find a Japanese to marry you? was her mother's response, while Heinrich was present. Heinrich, who spoke Japanese fluently. He laughed it off, but later, when Makiko tried to apologise for her mother, his lips made a thin line of displeasure, a sign which she came to know well later.

Oba Kikue was her mother's only sister, but they did not speak to each other. Makiko's mother would not be drawn on the subject, no matter how many

194

approaches Makiko made. She did, however, allow Makiko to spend holidays there, for appearance's sake. Oba Kikue, when pressed, would only say that it was her own fault she had been cast out because she, a woman, said what she thought, and this made her an anomaly and an embarrassment to Makiko's mother, and especially to Makiko's father.

And now there are two of them, two outcasts and a small boy, living alone, keeping to themselves. They are not nuns, but they might as well be.

Oba Kikue claims that she prefers to use the garden to grow the vegetables and fruits which are so expensive to buy, but as these are usually failed attempts – her Oba does not have the *green fingers* – Makiko does not feel guilty about it.

The birds have already begun singing, though as yet there is still only a suggestion of the light which will soon illuminate the distant mountains; pale yellow streaks through the pewter sky. Makiko draws her woollen shawl around her. There is a coolness in the air, but she welcomes the return to the routine that the cooler weather brings: her Oba Kikue back at her teaching job, Kane back to school.

Lately, Kane has been . . . difficult. No longer pliable.

Without noticing, she has raked the gravel sea into

stormy, irregular waves. Makiko rises from her knees and goes back into the house.

In her Oba's simple bathroom she strips and pours water over her body from a long-handled wooden scoop. She does not mind that it is cold. It feels more pure. She dries herself and dresses and fixes her hair so every strand is in place. She does not wash when she first rises from bed, worried that she might wake Oba Kikue, who needs her sleep for her job, or Kane, who needs his sleep for his practice.

But now it is time to wake him.

Kane grumbles but, to Makiko's relief, this morning he gets up without too much persuasion. She gives silent thanks once more for the routine of school. She has rice waiting, and miso soup; she watches as he lifts the bowl to his mouth. They never speak before morning practice. Makiko thinks that to speak would break the spell of the dream world, that by not speaking she is allowing Kane's fingers to draw with them some of the magic from that realm. She does not know Kane's reasons. Does he, too, feel the power in maintaining the silence? Does he feel the magic? Perhaps he is simply tired.

At the piano, he yawns, then he begins. Scales. Makiko sits by the window. Her ear knows mistakes. Only mistakes. In June he came second in the Pan-Pacific Young Musician. That is why he must practise even longer, an extra hour in the morning, an extra hour at night. Second place is no place at all. This is what Makiko believes, and Makiko is Kane's manager. First place in the competition means guaranteed entry to the Academy with full scholarship.

Although their divorce agreement states that Heinrich will make child-support payments until Kane is eighteen, Makiko worries endlessly about money. She cannot work because it would interfere with the progress of Kane's career. Besides, there is no work for which she is suitable any longer, unless she becomes some old man's *office flower,* to be admired for her smile and what she wears, rather than for any work she might do. Sometimes she cannot prevent the pain of regret from infusing her thoughts, regret that she could not make Heinrich happy, that he did not stay with her and Kane in Chicago. She could have a proper job, teaching Japanese. Heinrich had tried to persuade her, but she put him off. After Kane is settled in school, she bargained. But it was not Kane. It was her. Why could she not overcome her timidity, her fear of her new city? In Kyoto, she was not timid.

Kane's teacher was reluctant to agree to the new regime.

—He must not sprain, must not overdo, he said when Makiko told him. Kane's teacher also suffered from anxiety. Sadly, it had spoiled his career as a musician, but for Makiko, for Kane, it was fortuitous, for how else would they have found so talented a

197

teacher, and right here in their own district. In the end he agreed to the extra practice time. On a trial basis. He sounded weary as he said it.

Kane is playing the opening bars of his technical demonstration piece. For most of her son's life she has been listening to Bach. But it is only recently that she has begun to wonder: what is Bach to her? He is nothing to her, is the answer she finds. He is clever and Western and alien, just like her clever German husband.

Kane plays Bach well, she has been told. She can hear it herself, his confidence in the clear, intelligent progressions. It is his birthright, after all. And always a requisite part of his programme, at whatever level. Yet it occurs to her that she uses Bach. Bach, and Handel, and Beethoven. She uses them all as weapons against her husband. She will never define him as *ex,* as he is and always will be her only husband, though she did not allow him to become the digger of her grave. When she communicates Kane's progress to him, via email, she tells him that Kane plays Bach beautifully, that one day he will hear Kane play at Carnegie Hall. She does not read his replies. His new life, wife, son, she does not wish to know about.

Kane has stopped playing. It is time to get ready for school already. Lost in her thoughts, she may even have slipped into a doze while he was playing. It is happening more and more. The closer her patience and persistence come to paying off, the more blurred become the lines between waking and sleeping, so her days seem dreamlike to her.

—Kane's bus, Oba Kikue calls from the bathroom, breaking the spell the morning has cast. Come, Kane, you do not want to be late. Makiko, we are low on soy milk. Can you go to the store? Coffee too.

Makiko permits herself a smile. Coffee, so expensive here in Japan, is her Oba's sole indulgence.

—Coming, Oba, she replies, rising. Is there anything else?

Oba Kikue is wearing her navy skirt and an understated white blouse, and her hair, streaked with whites, is gathered into a coil at the nape of her neck: every inch the respectable schoolteacher. Yet there is the ineluctable hint of amusement in her eyes, suggesting another side to her, the side that has kept her from advancing in her career, probably kept her from marriage too. Makiko has seen how Oba Kikue frightens men.

—A couple of bottles of sake, perhaps. It is the weekend, after all. We can let our hair down. Oba Kikue keeps her face completely straight.

Makiko is still smiling after they leave.

After the energy of the young boy and the lively Oba, stillness falls over the house once more. This is Makiko's life. She has full mornings, household business to attend to, and business concerning Kane. Today, for example, she must liaise with Kane's teacher.

She switches the computer on, and sets the kettle to boil for tea. Lately, there is a wisp of discontent blowing around the edges of her days, like mist. It is there now, as the house falls still. It is there also at night, before she sleeps. It curls around her waist and hips and snakes itself between her thighs. It is in her dreams, and when she wakes, it is with the unsettling knowledge that while she slept her leaves have been rustled, her gravel disturbed. Then she can no longer sleep. Earlier and earlier, she creeps out to her garden, as if by kneeling on guard she can keep the impending changes at bay.

Dear Mr Yamamoto. The telephone would be quicker, more direct, but she prefers email. She can control what she says and, to some extent, what Kane's teacher says in response. There was a time . . . Foolishness. His, in particular. When Kane first began lessons, the teacher, Mr Yamamoto – Makiko refused his repeated entreaties to call him Kenichi – tried to strike up a friendship. He knew she was married. Her situation, returned from her marriage to a Westerner and bringing her child, was not unusual. He knew, yet still he was over-friendly, enthusiastic about how much Kane had learned, asking so many questions about the methods of his other teacher, things that no longer mattered.

Mrs Martello, the great, lumbering woman who was always so kind yet seemed so lonely, who channelled through slow, plump fingers the magic her mother had taught her.

—Mrs Martello had no method, Makiko told Mr Yamamoto.

—Then she was a very gifted teacher, he replied. And Kane is a very gifted boy. Let us hope we will have as much success as this Mrs Martello.

It was one of the arguments with Heinrich, the question of Kane's talent. Heinrich was in favour of music, but he wanted it to be *fun*. This was because as a graduate student he had lived in the United States, where everything is supposed to be fun. But fun did not lead to excellence. Only hard work and perseverance led to excellence. Surely he knew this from his own experience; his own sacrifices to gain his university position, his precious tenure.

—Hard work, and *talent*, he said bitterly. Was he suggesting Kane was without sufficient talent to succeed? She did not reply that morning in Chicago, but lifted his arm from her waist and got out of their bed to wake Kane for his morning practice. It was to be one of their last mornings.

—It is not a question of hoping, Makiko told Mr Yamamoto. It is a question of hard work and perseverance.

Mr Yamamoto nodded and got on with the lesson. After, when he stood and stretched, his shirt pulled out of his waistband, exposing a small area of taut brown skin, Makiko lowered her eyes, but not before he saw her notice.

—Can I get you something to drink? Perhaps Kane would like—

—Kane wants for nothing. Come, Kane. Mr Yamamoto, until next lesson, thank you.

And, with a small bow, she was gone.

In these matters, one needed only to be business-like, she told Oba Kikue later, but her Oba's smile looked a lot like pity. Marriage might be a woman's grave, but it seemed being alone was not good either. But Makiko was neither married, not really, nor was she alone. She had Kane, and she had Oba Kikue. She was content. She wanted for nothing.

Her fingers tap the computer keyboard, rhythmic and error-free, outlining the schedule Kane has been working on; the goals he is working towards; what his, Mr Yamamoto's, part is to be. Before her concluding salutation, she hesitates, undecided whether or not she will mention Kane's recent mutinies. *I hate Bach! I hate you!* She decides against. It is for her to control her son. It will take more hard work, continued perseverance, but she has an obligation to him, and to his talent. She clicks *Send* with an uneasy feeling.

They like to talk, the storekeepers. Makiko exchanges as few words as she can get away with without seeming impolite. She is relieved when she escapes them. So much work to do, she tells herself as she scurries back home. So much sweeping, so much cleaning.

But all too soon she has completed her tasks for the day, and still it is several hours before her Oba and Kane will return. She casts about for some occupation, and her eye settles on the oven. Of course. Green-tea sponge cake. Kane will be pleased. She sets out her ingredients and begins measuring, pouring and whisking, and soon the house is filled with the smell of baking. She is humming as she eases the soft yet firm cake from its tin and leaves it to cool on the wire rack.

At last she hears footsteps on the path. Kane bursts through the door, dropping bags and coat and kicking off his shoes, so tall and handsome and full of life. Makiko's heart swells at the sight of him.

—Kane. Come. I have made cake. You can have a slice before your practice, though it is still a little warm for cutting.

His noisy entrance comes to a sudden silence, and out of the silence the wisp of mist floats in front of her face so she cannot see clearly, and wraps itself loosely around her throat so she cannot call out. Involuntarily, she thinks of Heinrich, because in that moment she knows what it is like to lose a son.

Kane's disembodied voice reaches her as if from a distance.

—I promised Daichi I would go to his house to play soccer.

Then there is more clatter; her Oba's voice, and the inaudible sound of her Oba absorbing the atmosphere into which she has arrived. When the fog thins, Makiko can see her Oba looking from Kane to her, sees her take in the baking smells, weighing all this against the routine of the house. She smiles at Kane, then at Makiko.

—I take it you two do not agree on something?

Makiko holds down the fear and anger as she might hold in vomit until she can reach a toilet. She nods.

—Kane?

—I promised Daichi I would go over to play soccer, he repeats.

—If you promised, Oba Kikue says mildly, then you must go.

Kane does not understand at first, and then he does understand. He races out the door without looking at his mother.

—The boy cannot be forced, her Oba says.

She is her Oba, her elder, and Makiko cannot, is

not entitled to, reply. Makiko walks quickly out of the house to her garden where she sits and tries to pay attention to her rake and her stones, but her heart is erratic, her breathing ragged. The gravel patterns elude her.

Inside, the green-tea sponge lies, cool now and untouched. Kane is gone, and her Oba has retired to her bedroom, where she likes to read and rest after work.

—O.

Makiko puts her hand to her mouth to cover her exclamation because she realises for the first time that this arrangement exists because she has commandeered the sole living space for Kane and his practice.

So much sacrificed by so many. For Kane.

Six years earlier, Kane had only just started at elementary school when he brought home the note. There would be a bake-sale, a fundraiser for the school. All contributions were welcome.

—You will meet the other mothers, Heinrich said. But she knew she would not. She found even the most simple interactions impossibly difficult. She did what she had to, such as meeting with Kane's teacher, Miss Delorente, to ensure that he was on track with his school work, and taking him across town to his piano lesson each week. But she had to work hard to psychologically prepare herself to do these things. She did them for Kane. But chatting with other mothers? It was impossible.

—I will make my green-tea sponge, she told Kane. It was his favourite, and one of the few desserts she knew how to make.

Kane did not have the courage to ask her himself. That was the worst part of it all. He was afraid he would hurt her feelings. Instead, he asked his father to ask for him: he wanted to bring cookies. Bobby's Mom was making cookies.

—Something they recognise, Heinrich tried to persuade her in his most reasonable voice. It will make it easier to fit in, Kiko.

Maybe it was his calling her Kiko, which he knew she did not like. Maybe it was his reasonable voice. Maybe it was that nothing was a problem for Heinrich. He had no difficulty fitting in, with his fluent English and his coffees with his colleagues, while she was alone at home, all her focus on Kane. Maybe it was his need to fit in, for her to fit in, for Kane to fit in to this loud, lumpen culture she wanted no part of. Kane would not fit in, he would rise far above.

Or maybe it was that she knew about his affair. One of his smirking Western graduate students. She had learned about it months before but decided to keep her humiliation private, hoping that the affair would burn itself out. The note was the tipping point, the *mothers* were the tipping point. *Kiko* was the tipping point. Makiko lost control over herself for a first and only time, in a most shameful manner; shouting, throwing, even slapping. Heinrich did not try to stop her, or even to protect himself, and when her fury wore itself out and she fell, exhausted, onto the sofa, he told her that he could not leave the student, his girlfriend. He wanted to, but he could not, because she was expecting a baby.

The next day he moved out, and in the evening Makiko made green-tea sponge for the bake-sale, quietly and methodically, while Kane slept. When he came down in the morning and saw the cake cooling he tried to hide his disappointment, but Makiko said

—Close your eyes, and she took from the cupboard the Betty Crocker box she had purchased the day before. Open it, she said. Ta-da!

They followed the instructions together to create a tray of American cookies with chocolate chips like dried mouse droppings and decorated with sprinkles. Kane carried them carefully to school, to the top table, presided over by Miss Delorente.

—They're beautiful, she said. Did you make them, Kane? He nodded proudly, and stepped to one side for Makiko, who followed behind, carrying her green-tea sponge in shaking hands.

—If that's Japanese green-tea cake it's my absolute favourite, she said.

Kane looked anxiously at his mother, wondering if she had understood the English.

Makiko gave a small bow. She understood. It was the confidence to speak that she lacked.

—It's my favourite too, Kane said shyly, and Makiko thought the smile he gave her might break her heart.

Later that year she took Kane out of his school and, without telling Heinrich, who was busy with his mistress and new baby, returned to Japan. Kane was pliable then. He would adjust easily, she told herself on the flight. She took a cab to her mother's house, knowing her father – he was still alive then – would be at work. She explained that Heinrich had had an affair, that he never understood how important it was to nurture Kane's talent, that it was for the best that she had come home. Her mother listened in silence. When Makiko had finished, her mother said

—A woman must stay with her husband.

—But—

—No *but*, her mother snapped. This is what you learned in America? To disrespect your elders?

—No, Haha. Makiko bowed her head and was silent.

Her mother said she had brought shame on the

family. Said she was damaged goods, seconds, and that no man would want her now. Said she would struggle her whole life just to survive. Said that sometimes one must put up with a situation that is not to one's liking for the sake of one's child. She said she could not stay. The shame would kill her father.

Makiko did not tell her mother that she wanted no other man, or that Heinrich had made provision for Kane, or that she thought her father would not be ashamed of her. Instead, she left and boarded a train to Kyoto, hoping desperately that Oba Kikue would take her and Kane in.

She returned to her mother's house once, when her father died two years later.

—You did it, her mother told her, and closed the door to her.

She has not returned.

She does not know what to do with the cake. There is a steady pressure, rising up in her like the carbon dioxide bubbles in water that has stood still for a long time. Were she to give in to it, she would take the cake and throw it with her full force against the ricepaper walls. Then she would throw herself at the same walls until she, or they, broke. She imagines herself sliding, defeated, onto the floor. Then what would her future hold? What would her mother do, what would Japan do with a damaged woman? And Kane? Where would Kane be? Who would guard Kane's talent?

She opens a cupboard and removes a plastic container. From a drawer she takes a roll of grease-proof paper. She cuts the paper neatly to fit the box, then she lines it and places the cake inside. She covers it with the lid and presses around the edges, listening for the click that lets her know it is airtight.

2027

Bellis

The man at the desk looks around a hundred years old. Bellis is about to ask where she can find a list of former miners but as she approaches he waves her on into the museum.

If he's anything like Nana, he's sparing them both an ordeal of miscommunication. Nana will pretend to understand a question. *Is there a draught on you, Nana? Ah no, love, I just had a cup.* She won't wear her HearClear, says it's like listening to things that were never meant to have a sound, and those fellows above in their laboratories might be clever but they have no sense. She made Bellis put it on, and even with the volume right down she knew what Nana meant. Sitting still, she could hear her shoes creaking. She could hear her own heartbeat, and Nana's, and the two were out of sync. It made her breathless. She's told Mum to lay off Nana about the HearClear, not that it does much good. Mum confuses sporadic nagging with actual caring.

Another geriatric appears through a door marked *Private*. This one is only, oh, about eighty.

—Can I help you, Ma'am?

It's weird, being called Ma'am by someone who could be your grandfather.

—I'm looking for a list of miners who worked here?

—Right over here, Ma'am.

He crosses to the back wall, surprisingly sprightly for an old guy, to a plaque with a long list of names and dates carved into granite. Beside it, a huge panel of glass separates visitors from what used to be the mine shaft. In the glass she sees their reflection, an elderly man followed by a young woman with slouching shoulders. She steps to one side, afraid it might give her vertigo to look down.

—A relative, Ma'am?

—My grandfather.

—Is he . . . ?

There's a glimmer of hope in his clear grey eyes. A glance shows that the dates go way back to the middle of the last century. Is he still alive? he's asking.

—He died a long time ago. I was very young. He worked here in the 1950s.

No one believes her when she says she remembers Grandad. Maybe what she remembers are the photos and stories, and how everything changed after he died. Her mum divorced her dad, for starters. Then there was that holiday. That's why it felt so familiar when the plane landed in O'Hare yesterday. She only remembers bits; a dirty old farmhouse, some guy with a beard, bats . . . She shudders at the surfacing memories. Jesus, what was her mum thinking? They didn't stay there long. Funny how Mum didn't mention it when this trip came up, but she might've just forgotten about it too.

The old curator's smile is sad, far-away, as if he is already partially gone from this life.

—You're still very young, honey, he says, forgetting to be official. I'll give you some privacy. If you have any questions, I'll be right over here.

He moves away, straight-backed as a soldier.

She already knows she'll find the name; she's done the research. She doesn't need privacy. Take a photo, buy a souvenir. Done. Maybe she'll ask the old guy to take a photo of her standing beside the plaque, for Nana. This trip isn't necessary, but when she let it slip that she was trying to write about Grandad's mining days for the application, Nana got all excited. She insisted Bellis had to see the mine for herself, if the story was going to be any good. *Worth a shite*, is how she actually put it. Nana's language has gone to hell lately. Mum says it's probably the start of dementia, but Bellis thinks that since Uncle Kevin went to Mountjoy she can't be bothered with what people think anymore. Maybe it runs in the family.

Nana even wanted to come. Apparently she's been trying to get Mum to bring her for years.

College is Nana's idea too. Bellis can't expect to freelance forever. Between the lines, Bellis hears *freeload*. She writes content for company websites, something that grew out of her blog years ago, but it doesn't pay regularly or much. If she had to pay rent, she'd be screwed. Nana's trying to convince her to get a piece of paper, make something of herself. Only Bellis can't even motivate herself to fill out the application form. It's all personal essays and *tell us about yourself*, stuff she's not comfortable with. Give her a brief – banking, logistics, export statistics, whatever – and she'll give you back a succinct piece of writing, but this shit . . .

She can't deny, it'd be a lot of fun having Nana here. But when she fractured her hip and couldn't come, Bellis had to admit she was more relieved than disappointed. Last night would've panned out differently, too.

The trip isn't necessary, but as her finger touches the stone and trails slowly down the names a shiver runs through her, as if she's reading the past through her finger tips, like braille.

The hotel was way better than she expected, all sleek marble and glass. Her mum booked it with her air miles, but she never said how fancy it was. Her room on the twenty-second floor was huge, with windows overlooking the city. Careful to keep her eye at roof level to avoid the dizzying shafts between the buildings, she could even make out a tiny corner of lake. Even better, a quick rummage through the cupboards and drawers turned up a well-stocked minibar.

But though she'd been up since four, here the day was just beginning. She was used to packing in as much as possible when she travelled – legacy of her mum – so she headed out to do some sightseeing. By the time she had ticked off Choose Chicago's Top Ten, her feet were on fire and she was looking forward to a long bath, followed by that big, white bed.

The revolving door swept her in from the hot, noisy street, turned her soundlessly around and released her gently into the cool, citrus-scented lobby. It was as if the change in air went straight to her head, like high altitude does, and her plans for the evening vaporised. Instead of going straight to her room, her feet, without instruction, whispered her across to one of the white leather sofas, where a waiter floated to her side with the murmured suggestion of *a Martini, or a Bellini, or maybe Madam would prefer a dry white wine?*

In minutes her parched tongue was quenched with an astringent Pinot Gris, and her palate sated by the bitter green olives which came with it. Her hand wrote the room number she didn't know she'd memorised on the slip he offered. After a few sips, the alcohol began to do its work. Bellis was one of those tense people who other people like to tell *You should try yoga. Or Tai Chi. Or hot stones.* She preferred tequila. Or wine. Or whatever. But try telling that to the hot stone people. She took another sip, relishing the fact that she was on her own. She liked being on her own. It was just as well, really. If it wasn't for Nana, she'd rarely be any other way. Nana lives with them now, which means she puts up with Mum until Mum drives her mad with her nagging, then she comes out to Bellis in the converted garage for respite and a good bitch about Mum.

Plenty of people moved through the lobby, to and from their rooms. She was fond of people-watching, just not people-interacting. Two receptionists with matching straight blonde hair and demure white blouses resided behind a semi-opaque white desk, never seeming to speak above a whisper. And there was a pianist, Asian-looking, wearing a white tuxedo,

218

playing a white grand piano. She hadn't noticed him when she first came in.

The tune was something classical, except he was playing it like slow jazz, and she found herself keeping time. Not so anyone would notice, not foot tapping or finger clicking, that wasn't her style. It was more like her blood, her bone marrow . . . It was ridiculous, but it felt like her actual organs were pulsing to his touch.

She was not normally *in tune* with herself. But at the exact moment when she realised this, he forced her to look over and meet his eyes. At least, that was what it felt like. It was probably just the wine. Acting unlike herself, she rose and moved across the lobby to the small platform where he played. It was only as she got nearer that she noticed how grubby her trainers were and how maybe her top smelt a bit. She wished she had taken that bath first, and had floated down to the lobby wearing something . . . floaty . . . and maybe not black, though a quick inventory reminded her that there was nothing floaty in her bag, and nothing not black.

He closed the lid of the piano abruptly, interrupting her reverie, and stood and stretched and yawned loudly, at odds with the near-celestial lobby. The receptionists looked up in startled unison. He mimed smoking a cigarette. To them? Her? The receptionists glanced at each other with matching expressions. Clearly they did not approve. No one does. Cigarettes are illegal here, same as at home. The fines are huge. He strolled through the lobby and past the receptionists, and she didn't understand this bit but she followed him, past the elevators and down a long corridor, which grew less heavenly with every turn, until they came to a fire door, *For Use in Emergencies Only*. He pushed the bar down and they went through, into a small interior yard containing skips full of rubbish. She felt instantly less grubby and more at home, despite her angelic companion in his white suit.

—So, he said.

—So, she said.

He took a white plastic box from his jacket pocket, flipped open the top and removed a cigarette, before offering one to her. She accepted. She practised this dark art when she could. It was why her favourite haunts were the underground kind. If she ever felt at ease in company, this was the time: after a couple of drinks, her hands cupped loosely around a cigarette, waiting to get a light. His lighter was built into the box, with a small button on the underside, and a safety catch so he wouldn't accidentally set himself alight. Cool. She'd have to try and smuggle one of them home. He held it in long, stained fingers until she got an orange glow going, then he lit his own. Together, they pulled the smoke into their bodies, then exhaled long, contented sighs.

—So, he said again. Who are you?

—Bellis.

He took another drag.

—I'm Kane. One more hour and I'm done, he said through a little series of inhalations.

She nodded. She'd take a bath, meet him back in the lobby.

But instead of going up to her room like she should have, she went back to her seat, ordered another Pinot Gris, and let his music wash over and through her. Running along with the notes were lines of a poem, which she tried to ignore. Spouting poems was an affectation too far. Grandad was always one for a recitation, though, and this trip was supposed to be about him. Or did she really remember that? Was she just repeating what Mum had told her, or Nana? Then why was she murmuring to herself about *green waters of the canal* and something about redemption? She ordered another drink, and then another. Pinot Gris, *pouring redemption for me.* She'd go and have that bath soon.

But the jet lag must have had more of an effect than she'd thought, because when she stood to leave her legs weren't ready. He appeared beside her before she'd even noticed that the music had stopped, his hand firm beneath her elbow, steadying her. Two blonde heads turned to watch them as they walked to the elevator.

She shrugged him off when the elevator stopped at her floor, and let herself into her room. He followed, kicked off his shoes, and went past her. He picked up the stick and pointed it. *Welcome, Bellis,* declared the screen. *Please enter your code.* He put it down and threw off his jacket, then his bow tie. His shirt followed and, wearing just a white T-shirt and trousers, he stretched himself out on the big bed like it was his hotel room. He yawned again.

—So?

Bellis prided herself on sleeping with guys she barely knew and would never see again. This meant Erasmus students, rugby fans, guys on stag parties. So what was stopping her peeling her T-shirt off as she had so many times before, revealing her better than adequate breasts, holding his gaze as she unwound her plait and let her hair fall, watching his prick rise to the occasion, as pricks always do?

—I'm going to take a shower, she told him. 2-0-0-5-*B-E-L-L-I-S*, if you want to browse.

He grinned.

—Year of birth, name? Exactly what they tell you not to use?

—Exactly.

She turned to hide her smile and went into the bathroom, pulling the door behind her. When it didn't close fully, she left it. She stripped off her travel clothes and turned on the shower. Before she stepped under the cascade of hot water she turned a slow 180 degrees, to give him a bit of a show. In the bathroom mirror she could see him, watching.

He was still there when she emerged, damp and naked. He looked as if he hadn't moved. Nor did he make any move now, seeming content just to watch her. She glanced, and yes, there was the tell-tale bulge in his pants. What was he waiting for?

Pretending to ignore him, she went to the minibar, still naked, and took out a tiny bottle. Gin.

—Want something? she asked, twisting off the lid. She perched awkwardly on the edge of the desk, but she knew she looked good with her damp tendrils trailing over her breasts, a wanton mermaid.

He shook his head.

—I don't drink.

—Suit yourself.

This guy was starting to annoy her. What was he even doing in her room? She tilted the small bottle into her mouth and emptied it in one, shuddering slightly at the sharp taste.

—Bellis, he said. Unusual.

She never told any of these guys anything about herself, and so far this guy wasn't even one of these guys. Actually, she never tells anyone anything about herself. Her mum's counsellor said it was because her father had left at such a crucial stage in her development. Mum brought her there after she'd spent two days and nights wandering around Dublin without telling anyone where she was. She was about twelve or thirteen, when everything kicked off.

—She won't open up to me, Mum complained. I never know what she's thinking.

It didn't seem to occur to either of them that they were expecting her to *open up* to a complete stranger.

—*Abandoned* her, Mum corrected then, smug because it was Dad's fault, at which point the counsellor added that all the travelling would have been a contributing factor too. As programme manager at the University School of Nursing, Mum's job when Daisy was growing up involved travelling the globe, canvassing international students for their high fees, but rather than leave Daisy at home, she insisted on bringing her everywhere she went. It didn't matter how often Nana offered to take her, her mum wouldn't let her out of her sight. Daisy learned to become invisible in the corners of office meetings or at work dinners, lost in the parental-controlled virtual worlds of her computer.

—A child needs roots, and a network of friends, the counsellor finished in her preachy voice.

Yeah, right.

Neither of them was keen to go back after that, but Mum got way worse, monitoring Bellis's every move. She even changed jobs so they could be home more, now that Bellis was starting secondary school, and insisted on dropping her right at the school gate every morning.

She had a friend from school, sort of, Maraid. They had stuff in common. Absent parents, for one. Maraid's parents shared custody, which meant neither of them knew where she was or what she was doing half the time. Which was, mitching school with Bellis. School was the only place Mum couldn't follow her, so some days, instead of going to first period, Maraid and Bellis would head into town, hang around the shops, steal stuff they felt like having, or just because it was something to take: clothes, make up, that sort of thing. After school, Bellis would call to say she was staying over at Maraid's to study, and Mum couldn't do anything about it because, after all, the counsellor had prescribed friends. They'd go into town to pubs they knew were full of older men, probably married, usually overweight and all with wallets full of cash, because it wouldn't do to put overpriced wine and food onto their cards for their wives to see. Bellis and Maraid would sit on their knees, let them buy drinks all evening, then go with them to their apartment or hotel room and have sex with them.

The first time, they dared each other. Losing their virginity was high on their to-do list. They picked up two guys, some salesman from England for Bellis, his cousin for Maraid. When he finished and let his weight collapse onto her, crushing her skinny bones to the bed and looking like he planned to fall asleep, she pushed him off and ran to the next room to tell Maraid. She was on her own. The cousin had found out her age and done a runner. She was sick with jealousy. *Go wake my guy*, Bellis told her. In the end they went in together giggling and climbed in either side of him. He was happy to oblige. They were fifteen.

They drifted apart when Maraid got an actual boyfriend. Bellis was careful never to let that happen to her. If she had to speak to the men she picked up, she told them that she was a student nurse, or a vet, or a pilot. That her parents were killed in a plane crash. Or a safari accident. Or by long, slow cancers. That she was a trust-funder. Or a bankrupt. That her name was Jill, or Queeva, or Candy.

But a glance at Kane told her he didn't care what her name was. Maybe his wasn't even Kane. She leaned in to the minibar and extricated another small bottle.

—It's short for Bellis Perennis. Aka Daisy, she said.

He looked confused.

—Latin, for *daisy*. Cute for a baby, a toddler, a little girl. Perfect design concept for a little-girl bedroom, a little-girl dress. Spot on for a white flower with a yellow centre. But ridiculous for a teenager, and downright irresponsible to inflict it on someone who would someday become a full-grown woman. I changed it.

—Ah, he nodded. Then he frowned. *Bellis* is not a whole lot better, is it?

She shrugged.

—I was sixteen.

—Daisy. Daze. Did anyone call you Daze?

Was this guy trying to touch nerves? Well, she would hold hers. The guy on the farm, she remembered now. It really bothered her Mum. Probably because the only other person to call her Daze was . . . Despite her resolve, she had to swallow.

—My dad.

The two words dropped into the conditioned air and hung there.

—You get along with your dad? Kane asked, as oblivious to her discomfort as he seemed to be to her body.

—They divorced when I was three. He bored her to death. Or that's what she told me when she'd had a few glasses of wine once. Then he met some woman, got her pregnant, went to live in London. End of.

—Is that where he lives now, London?

—Now? No, that was years ago. Now, he lives in

Bali. Has two more little girls. Two different mothers. One of them's my age. The mothers, I mean.

Kane's face was expressionless. She didn't know why she was trying to shock him. Maybe because all that white made him look unshockable. Maybe because she was sitting here, tits out, and he wasn't budging.

—They all live together in the same compound. He rents surfboards to tourists.

—And your mum divorced him because he was boring?

She failed to suppress a smile.

He sat up and swung long legs over the side of the bed.

—Come on. Let's go see Chicago. He paused, as if he was only now noticing her state of undress.

—Maybe you should put something on first.

He threw his discarded shirt at her and she caught it, splashing vodka onto it in the process.

—Good reflexes.

—Thanks.

Because she couldn't think of any reason not to, she put the shirt on, rolling the sleeves to fit.

—Looks good on you.

—Are you from Chicago? she asked, ignoring him. It'd be cool to see Chicago with someone local. She didn't tell him she'd spent all day sightseeing already.

He shrugged, like he either didn't know, or didn't care.

—I live here. I guess I'm from here, he said at last. He already had the door open.

The Chicago she'd seen earlier did not include the seedy, noisy streets he took her to, lit by stuttering neon, punctuated by a sudden wedge of noise from an open door. Intimidating-looking bouncers hung around outside bars and clubs, women staggered by in unimaginable heels and hair and nails. He took her hand and walked straight past a bouncer through a black metal door she hadn't seen. She only noticed how tall he was when they stood together at the bar. Under the lights she could see that his hair had a brownish hue. His eyes were Asian, but not brown, as she would have expected.

—What colour are your eyes anyway? she asked over the music.

—Green. He handed her a cocktail, also green.

—Me too.

She took a drink. It was vile.

—Fifty bucks a pop, he shouted.

For himself he had ordered what looked suspiciously like a glass of water.

—Do they pay you well?

—The hotel? I guess. It's not the only place I work. He drank his water down in one go. Tell me more about your dad.

As mistress of changing the subject, she recognised it when it happened. This guy was starting to get interesting.

—Nothing more to tell, she said, and it was her turn to get busy with her drink. As the green potion went down she could feel the throbbing bass pass through her feet and up her spine to the beginnings of a familiar headache at the back of her skull.

—What about your mom? he asked.

—Let's leave that one alone. Unless you want to put me in a very bad mood. What about your mum?

As Kane balanced up her question, he looked like someone she knew very well. In the dim, drunk, reptilian part of her brain she began to understand something about him, about herself. Maybe it would come to her when she sobered up.

—My mother lives in Japan, he shouted. Quietly.

She conjured the usual mishmash of kimonos and tea ceremonies and cherry blossoms, despite real memories of elaborately automated toilets, meals in McDonald's and a lot of hotel rooms. She said nothing.

—My mother wanted a star. She devoted her life to my career.

He was looking into the bottom of his empty glass as if he might find another, happier version of his life there. He went on.

—I was on track. Right up to the moment I figured

out it was a track I didn't want to be on. Why would anyone want to be a classical pianist? A few glorious hours on a stage, the rest of the time in some practice room with no windows, just so Mom can have bragging rights. There's no way it's worth it. Less pressure taking a job in an assembly line.

—But you didn't. Take a job on an assembly line, I mean.

—I did, he said. For a while. Putting small round parts into small round holes. But I couldn't stay away from music.

—So now you play in hotel lobbies.

He looked at her curiously, to see if she was putting him down. As if she was in any position to put anyone down.

—I guess. I play in clubs sometimes, real clubs.

—Like this one?

He looked around as if he had only just noticed where they were.

—Let's get out of here. Let me show you a real club.

He held out his hand, and by now she needed it.

—Kane? She had one more question, one more he wouldn't want to answer.

—Yeah?

—Did you break your mum's heart when you quit?

They were already pushing their way through the

crowd, so she couldn't see his face, but there was an adjustment to the muscle tension of his neck.

—Yeah, I guess I broke her heart, he said without turning around.

The Bone Yard was more bar than club, but it stayed open all night, and it had live music. A trio was playing something intense and jazzy. People sat at small tables around the edge of the tiny dance floor in semi-darkness, some talking and drinking but most listening to the band. A few people greeted Kane by name as they made their way through. He found a table, then brought two bottles of mineral water from the bar. So he'd decided she'd had enough?

—This is Jay Jack. The guy on sax. He can hit notes you wouldn't believe. The guy on keyboards is really hot too. It's like he has a whole other rhythm all of his own. The rest of us are just running behind him, trying to keep up.

Us. Did Kane play with these guys? She didn't know much about music. Too busy shoplifting and skipping school to know much about anything that wasn't the content she wrote for other people's websites, and that was forgotten the moment she sent off the copy. She could feel herself begin to sober up which, given the amount of alcohol she'd drunk, was remarkable. It must be a side effect of jet lag.

She could make out the rhythm of the keyboard. It reminded her of the syncopated heartbeats from her nana's HearClear, only this time she didn't panic. She counted instead, trying to find the beat, but she couldn't get it. One two three, four five six, seven eight nine, ten eleven, one?

—Eleven?

—That's it.

His grin told her she'd just graduated to best girl in the class. It was the first time she'd ever wanted to be that.

They sat back and listened. When the other musicians began to withdraw, first with their music, then physically, moving towards the back of the little stage, the audience sat up a bit straighter, antennae out. Something big was about to happen.

—Get ready, Kane told her.

As his band members faded away, Jay Jack seemed to grow, in both sound and stature. Mouth and breath and polished brass melded into a sound that snaked itself around the little band of bodies lucky enough to have gathered there that night. When the sound overwhelmed the space until there wasn't room for any more, it began to build in tempo and volume, and Jay Jack was moving now as if led by his sax, onto the dance floor, towards the tables. He was so near they could see the gleam of sweat on his face, the gleam of candlelight on the brass. The sheer force of it, the joy of it, took her by surprise. She felt Kane's eyes on her and realised that she was crying. He was smiling when he leaned over and kissed her. It vibrated the whole way through her, along with the long-held final note of Jay Jack's solo.

Then he was taking her by the hand again, and they were cruising through the streets, dropping in and out of bars and clubs, a coffee shop, a fast-food place. There was more drink, more cigarettes. There were donuts, hot out of the oven. At some point they were walking by water, the lake, smoking weed. There were trains going past, drowning out the sound of their talk. When daylight made its appearance, she resented it for butting in.

Then they were on the white bed, fully clothed and not touching, the white ceiling a blank canvas above them. They'd said everything. His mom trying to control his life, never marrying again. Her mum trying to control her life, never marrying again. And all that travel. She could show him photos from Shanghai to St Petersburg, Rome to LA, Tel Aviv to Sydney, and everywhere in between if he liked. They were on MyPod.

He turned his head at that. Personal photos on public forums was universally frowned upon.

—Teenage rebellion?

She nodded.

—'Course. They're so paranoid. Like they have

any actual privacy. I decided to put it all out there when I was, oh, about . . .

—Thirteen?

—Yes. You too? I mean, it's not like I ever do anything especially strange. Put it all out there, every little mundane thing. Drown them, whoever *them* is, in information. So everything you want to know about Bellis Perennnis McCarthy is there for you, and them, to see. All you need's the code.

—2-0-0-5-B-E-L-L-I-S?

—That's it. Sometimes I think they're right, though. Not about privacy, more about what we're meant to remember. The way memory works, you know. Like, I completely forgot I'd been to Chicago before, until the plane landed today – or was it yesterday? It's like we're not supposed to remember so much about ourselves. That we forget stuff for a reason . . . Know what I mean?

—Sure, Kane said agreeably, but she could tell that he didn't. She didn't know exactly what she meant either. She picked up the stick and punched in her code. Kane propped himself up onto his elbows to see the screen.

—Let's see. Year . . . About . . . She pointed and scrolled.

There she was, a skinny pre-teen, poised to pick a bunch of bananas. There she was with a coconut. There she was with the ubiquitous straw in the now topped coconut. There was the brown man who had topped it, with his machete, glowering at the camera. She grinned.

—I took that one. Anyway, you get the idea.

Kane took the stick to browse some more.

—When we got back from our travels, I ran away. Just walked out the front door when I was supposed to be in bed and kept walking. I hadn't planned it or anything. Puberty was like waking up and discovering I'd been in jail my whole life, but the jailer had left the door open. When they found me, Mum got so paranoid that if she could have had me electronically tagged, she would have. And the worse she got, the worse I reacted. Skipped school, screwed up, screwed around.

She sneaked a glance to see his reaction, but there was none. He continued flicking back through the photos, a younger and younger Bellis. She hadn't looked at any of these in years.

—You know the rest. My nana thinks I should go to college. I'm supposed to be researching my grand-father. He was a miner over the border, in Canada. Thing is, it's my mum's story really. She's the one who should be going to Canada.

This had only just dawned on her. Her mum, in search of herself all across the world, when she should've started where her own dad started.

—Kiyomizu-dera, Kane said. He had paused at a

picture where Bellis, about eleven, stood with her mum on steps leading to a temple. Her mum's arm was around her waist, and she had a huge smile for whoever was taking the picture. Some passer-by, usually.

—What?

—The temple. It's near Kyoto, he said.

—Oh. Yea, that sounds right. I think we went there. Is that where you lived?

Kane nodded.

—It's where my mom lives now. With her broken heart. You should go to college, he added.

Like it was the most obvious thing in the world.

He was looking at another picture now: a little girl, barefoot, wearing a sleeveless, daisy-print dress. Bellis looked with him, with interest. She remembered. Those were strawberry plants. Those were hoophouses in the background. Mum taking the photo, the house behind her. The house with the bats, the bats in the attic. The attic . . .

Some things we're not supposed to remember.

She snatched the stick and turned it off, and just stayed staring at the blank screen. She didn't know she was trembling until Kane stood and pulled back the covers.

Here we go, she thought. Just another guy.

She pulled the shirt off to save him the trouble, but he put it back on over her head. Was he smothering her? Had she brought home one too many weirdos? He yanked it down over her torso, a straitjacket.

—You're gorgeous, he told her. But you're drunk, and you need some sleep. And you're shivering. Come here.

She had little choice but to push her arms into the sleeves. He pulled her down into the bed beside him and draped his arm loosely across her. It seemed an age before she could get warm again.

When she woke, he was sitting on the bed, watching her.

—What time is it? she croaked. Her cheek was stuck to the cotton sheet with dried drool.

He looked at his iWatch, an ancient thing she hadn't noticed yesterday, probably one of the first models. It suited him.

—Nine.

She groaned. Her head was throbbing.

—I have to go rent a car.

He waited for her to get up and showered. This time, she was fully clothed when she came out.

—Last night . . . she began. This was awkward. They weren't usually there the next day.

Kane put a finger to his lips.

—But I never got to ask . . .

He shrugged.

—Just, do you see your mum?

238

—It upsets her.

—What about your dad?

Time was running out. She had just minutes to find out everything about this guy who hadn't wanted to have sex with her. She needed enough facts to make him real, if she ever wanted to remember him.

—He lives here, he said.

He was already waiting by the door, his white dinner jacket thrown over his shoulder. Somehow the time for conversation had melted away with the arrival of the morning.

When they got to the lobby, he kissed her on the forehead.

—Thank you for spending the night with me, Bellis.

He was already gone before she had time to react, on his way out of the revolving doors. When his quadrant swung back around, empty, into the lobby, she swallowed down something that tasted like loss, and turned to reception. The receptionists did not look surprised that she had appeared with their resident pianist. He probably came down from a different room every day. What did she care? She was exactly where she would have been if Kane had not been playing piano in the lobby the previous evening, if she had gone straight up to her room, ordered room service and gone to sleep. So why did she feel like the last grain of sand had just fallen through her hourglass?

—Car rental? She forced brightness into her voice. Behind her, the door continued its slow revolutions.

Bellis's nomadic childhood has left its impression, and every time she has enough money accumulated, she gets on a plane. She has negotiated traffic in London and Manila, Mumbai and New York, and no matter how bad she's feeling, she's not about to let Chicago faze her. The satnav lady talks her seamlessly out of the city and onto the sedate Google lane, which will take her all the way to Canada. She tunes the radio to a local talk station, where an excitable host is interviewing Kim and Ken, two of the contestants from the latest UR-TV offering, where participants play Russian roulette with out-of-date canned food and wait to see who will get sick first. They're all vaccinated against everything, which seems to take all the fun out of it, but apparently sometimes a contestant contracts botulism anyway.

—Then let's talk about vaccinations instead, Bellis mutters. Jeez.

—Does anyone die? the host asks benignly.

—If that happens, Ken explains – I mean, no, but when anyone gets sick, they're treated right away. There's no actual suffering?

But he's beginning to sound doubtful.

—What about the rumours that one of the contestants [rustle of paper] . . . Brandy from Iowa, contracted a strain that was resistant to the treatment? And that she died as a direct result of Bottle It or Can It, specifically peaches dating back to 1989, and not a pre-existing heart condition, which was stated as the cause of death by UR-TV's legal team—

The host's voice turns to syrup.

—. . . Rumours, which I hasten to add, this station does not endorse? Or the ensuing litigation resulting from accepting a candidate with any pre-existing condition which might put them at risk. Are these rumours of any concern to you, Ken? Kim?

Now he's switched seamlessly into a business-like tone, like he's just asked them how they take their coffee. This guy is good. Ken and Kim stammer answers they hope will not get them kicked off the show.

The more inane the subject matter, the better it suits Bellis, and despite her queasy stomach she reaches the border with just two R&R stops. She gets out to stretch her legs before tackling the last stage of the drive. Her head feels tingly and disorganised, and her whole body is trembling slightly, still undecided about whether it wants to bottle or can the green brew and all the rest from last night.

She was worried the border police might give her a hard time, thinking she was some kind of druggie or something, but despite her shaking hand as she passed it across, her Irish passport gave her smooth passage.

—Got grandparents from there, the guard told her. The Emerald Isle.

—She smiled and nodded.

—You're welcome to Canada – he glanced at her passport – Bellis. He leaned closer. It's the Yanks we're trying to keep out, honey. Garcia's doin' his best, but the place went to hell with two terms of Gubanov, and we simply ain't got room for all of 'em up here.

She should eat something, but she wants to make it to Sudbury while it's still light. She has an itinerary to keep – Sudbury-Sleep-Museum-O'Hare – which she repeats like a mantra. She's reminded of Nana's plastic beads, creeping slowly through buckled, ancient fingers, the prayer a murmur on her barely-moving lips.

She gets back into the car.

Keep right, then take the next right onto Highway 17, the satnav tells her in a reassuring voice. Lake Huron is glittering on her right most of the way there, but she keeps her eyes fixed on the road ahead and drives a steady fifty all the way to her exit. Sudbury House, also booked by Mum, is clean and functional, and there's not a tuxedo in sight. She goes straight to bed and sleeps a long and dreamless sleep.

It's the kind of morning you know will get earth-cracking hot later, but in the pale yellow light and the cool air it's hard to think of this place as a wasteland. Trees line the streets, and she can see the glitter of another lake up ahead. There are three hundred in the area, according to her app. Well rested and more in control, she is feeling well disposed towards Sudbury.

The sun is gleaming off the highly polished surface of the doors, copper or bronze or something, as she approaches. But the blinds are drawn. Her optimism is already fading by the time she's close enough to read the small sign informing her of the museum's opening hours: *Afternoon only*. She does the quick calculation, though she doesn't really need to; it was already tight. If she waits for the museum to open, she'll miss her flight.

Out in front, a bronze miner stands, reflecting. He's part of a memorial to fallen miners. Bellis reflects with him. She can't come all the way here then not go in. Can she? She thinks about faking it for Mum and Nana. Surely the local stores would have souvenirs, postcards. She looks at the miner for guidance but he keeps his gaze fixed steadily ahead, thinking about his dead colleagues. Damn. She takes out her phone and scrolls to find the airline's site, hoping her mum will cover the overpriced, last-minute flight.

As she traces her finger over her grandfather's name – her name, too – she's glad she stayed. She remembers his hand, big and dry and cracked like the earth. At least one or two of her memories are not MyPod moments, they're her own, and she keeps them to herself. It's the only way she can be sure they're real. She remembers her small hand in his big safe hand, as he brought her down to the farmyard to show her the bales of straw where they were stacked as high as a house, and she's overcome with gladness to be here in this mine touching his name.

She takes a step closer to the mineshaft and it's as if she steps back in time. Her grandfather is standing where she is standing now, a young man not much older than she is, who knows nothing about the future, nothing about her. What is he thinking as he stands there on the threshold of the pit he will enter and out of which he will not emerge for four full years? She dares to look through the glass, down into the darkness, into her past and into herself, until she begins to feel dizzy with the whole swirling, percolating brew. Her breath is coming in short gasps, and a rush of the nausea she thought had abated suffuses her. She needs to sit down. There's a bench . . .

She takes the long slow breaths her GP taught her. When she lifts her head, the old man is beside her, holding out a glass of water.

—Feeling better, honey?

She takes the glass, mortified to have caused a scene.

—The past can do that sometimes, he says, like she's not the first visitor he's had to revive.

Canadian water is cold and sweet, and as it enters her body and becomes part of her, it gives her enough of its clarity to see that she's more than a hungover mess of Bellis Perennis Daisy Daze, she's a regular old tourist who's a bit fazed by the past, and this makes her feel better. She smiles up at him.

—Thank you.

—Sure, honey. Did you find what you were looking for?

He holds out his hand to take her empty glass.

Before she can settle on an answer, her phone buzzes with a message. Kane. Already, he feels like a dream from long ago. *Did you find what you were looking for?*

She looks at the outstretched hand. It's large and dry and cracked.

—Were you a miner?

—I was. I was a young man then, he says.

—I'd love . . . If you're not too busy . . . I'd love to hear about it, what it was like.

A broad grin spreads across his face, as if he's been waiting his whole life for someone to ask. Or maybe he's just bored. He offers his arm, and for an old man he's surprisingly strong.

—Come, it's more comfortable in the back. There's coffee. Old Albert's in there, mined in the fifties himself. You never know, he might even have known your grandpa. I'm John, by the way.

He thrusts that big hand out, the hand of history. In his big hand, hers feels warm and secure, and tiny as a child's.

—I'm Daisy.

—Pleased to make your acquaintance, Daisy.

When he says her name, everything goes fuzzy, like she's slipping between the present and the past, maybe even the future. As they walk to the back room, Daisy and the old miner, she thinks about Kane's message and whether she might even reply sometime.

Acknowledgements

Thanks are due to: Mark Richards and everyone at John Murray, who have been a pleasure to work with; Ger Nichol, my agent, for placing me there, and for her support at every stage of the process; everyone who read the manuscript at various stages and helped to make it better: my sister and put-upon first reader, Hilary McGrath; my clear-headed and kind MFA supervisor Lia Mills; Claire Coughlan, Andrea Carter, Henrietta McKervey, and all my MFA group at UCD; Carlo Gebler, our insightful writer-in-residence; James Ryan and Éilis Ní Dhuibhne for all their support, not just with this novel but all things writerly; to Mam, Alex, Georgia, Rafy and Mikey for keeping the faith; and not least to Tim, for support, patience and Insomnia coffee, and for not reading the early drafts.